THE WITCH AND THE GENTLEMAN

THE WITCH AND THE GENTLEMAN

The Witches Series Book 1
A Witches Novel

J.R. RAIN

ACCLAIM FOR THE NOVELS OF
J.R. RAIN:

"Be prepared to lose sleep!"
—**James Rollins**, international bestselling author of *The Doomsday Key* on J.R. Rain's *The Lost Ark*

"I love this!"
—**Piers Anthony**, bestselling author of *Xanth* on J.R. Rain's *Moon Dance*

"*Dark Horse* is the best book I've read in a long time!"
—**Gemma Halliday**, award-winning author of *Spying in High Heels*

"*Moon Dance* is a must read. If you like Janet Evanovich's Stephanie Plum, bounty hunter, be prepared to love J.R. Rain's Samantha Moon, vampire private investigator."
—**Eve Paludan**, bestselling co-author of *Witchy Business*

"Impossible to put down. J.R. Rain's *Moon Dance* is a fabulous urban fantasy replete with multifarious and unusual characters, a perfectly synchronized plot, vibrant dialogue and sterling witticism all wrapped in a voice that is as beautiful as it is rich and vividly intense as it is relaxed."
—**April Vine**, author of *Unbound*

"Is it possible to redefine two genres in one book? I don't know, but J.R. Rain has left a lasting impression for the vampire and mystery genres."
—**P.J. Day**, author of *The Sunset Prophecy*

OTHER BOOKS BY J.R. RAIN

STANDALONE NOVELS
The Lost Ark
Elvis Has *Not* Left the Building
The Grail Quest
The Body Departed
Silent Echo
Winter Wind

VAMPIRE FOR HIRE
Moon Dance
Vampire Moon
American Vampire
Moon Child
Christmas Moon
Vampire Dawn
Vampire Games
Moon Island
Moon River
Vampire Sun
Moon Dragon
Moon Shadow

JIM KNIGHTHORSE
Dark Horse
The Mummy Case
Hail Mary
Clean Slate
Night Run

THE WITCHES SERIES
The Witch and the Gentleman
The Witch and the Englishman
The Witch and the Huntsman
The Witch and the Wolfman

THE SPINOZA TRILOGY
The Vampire With the Dragon Tattoo
The Vampire Who Played Dead
The Vampire in the Iron Mask

THE VAMPIRE DIARIES
Bound By Blood

SAMANTHA MOON SHORT STORIES
Teeth
Vampire Nights
Vampires Blues
Vampire Dreams
Halloween Moon
Vampire Gold
Blue Moon
Dark Side of the Moon

JIM KNIGHTHORSE SHORT STORIES
Easy Rider

SHORT STORY SINGLES
The Bleeder

SHORT STORY COLLECTIONS
The Bleeder and Other Stories
Vampire Rain and Other Stories
The Santa Call and Other Stories

Co-Authored Books

COLLABORATIONS
Cursed (with Scott Nicholson)
Ghost College (with Scott Nicholson)
The Vampire Club (with Scott Nicholson)
Dragon Assassin (with Piers Anthony)
Dolfin Tayle (with Piers Anthony)
Jack and the Giants (with Piers Anthony)
Judas Silver (with Elizabeth Basque)
Lost Eden (with Elizabeth Basque)
Glimmer (with Eve Paludan)
The Black Fang Betrayal (with Multiple Authors)
The Indestructibles (with Rod Kierkegaard)

THE OPEN HEART SERIES
with Rod Kierkegaard
The Dead Detective

NICK CAINE ADVENTURES
with Aiden James
Temple of the Jaguar
Treasure of the Deep
Pyramid of the Gods

THE ALADDIN TRILOGY
with Piers Anthony
Aladdin Relighted
Aladdin Sins Bad
Aladdin and the Flying Dutchman

THE WALKING PLAGUE TRILOGY
with Elizabeth Basque
Zombie Patrol
Zombie Rage
Zombie Mountain

THE SPIDER TRILOGY
with Scott Nicholson and H.T. Night
Bad Blood
Spider Web
Spider Bite

THE PSI TRILOGY
with A.K. Alexander
Hear No Evil
See No Evil
Speak No Evil

THE WOLF PACK TRILOGY
with H.T. Night
Hungry Like the Werewolf
Running With the Werewolf
The Big, Bad Werewolf

The Witch and the Gentleman
Published by J.R. Rain
Copyright © 2013 by J.R. Rain
All rights reserved.

License Notes
This book is licensed for your personal enjoyment only. This book may not be re-sold or given away to other people. All rights reserved.

ISBN-10: 1502916983
ISBN-13: 9781502916983

DEDICATION

To Sandra, who keeps me sane.
Thank you for all that you do.

"It is on those mist-filled nights, when the wind is strong and curious, when the air is alive with something unseen but felt, that you finally believe…oh, yes, you finally believe what your heart has always known: *magic is real and it is everywhere.*"
—*Diary of a Pagan*

CHAPTER ONE

"Hi, this is Allison. Thank you for calling The Psychic Hotline. How can I help *you* see into the future?"

As I spoke and waited, I reached for my protein drink, which I had just whipped up a few minutes earlier. I found that protein drinks helped me connect with the spirits.

Yes, I'm a telephone psychic. A pretty good one, too. I'm also a personal trainer and hoped to someday start my own gym. A gym that focused on the body *and* the mind. Lofty dreams, but we all need them.

I set aside my protein drink, cleared my thoughts and glanced at my computer screen. According to my screen, I had a call on the line, a local number, too. I worked from home, plugged into my company's switchboard, so to speak. I wore headphones with a microphone, and as soon as I clicked on the number blinking on the screen, we were live.

The wonders of technology.

I adjusted my headphones. The previous callers were already out of sight, out of mind. A couple of kids wanted to mess with me. Except, of course, I sensed their names quickly enough to blow their minds. Then again, they were high and it wasn't very hard to blow their minds.

Yeah, we got a lot of jerks who liked to mess with us. It was part of the business. We also got a lot of people who needed real help. Little did the callers know they were getting a *real* psychic. A powerful psychic. One whose gifts were enhanced nearly daily, thanks to my unusual source of power. From a friend of mine who just happened to be a vampire.

Now, I focused on connecting my energy to the person on the other end of the line. I heard crackling in the background, followed by faint street noise.

It wasn't hard to connect with others on a psychic level once I learned how to do it. I practiced like a kid who had just learned how to ride a bike. It was a sort of mental *reaching out.* However, I knew it went further than just the mental. It was a brief connecting of souls. My soul connecting with the caller's. Except he didn't know I was connecting. Yes, I already knew it was a "he" on the other end of the line. And he had a very, very heavy problem weighing on his heart.

"Can you hear me?" asked a hesitant voice.

"Loud and clear," I said. "How can I help you?"

Through my living room's sliding glass door, the posh apartment building across the street caught some of the mid-afternoon sun, and glittered magnificently. A seagull swooped in that moment over my balcony, which was unusual because my Beverly Hills apartment was at least ten miles from the ocean.

"I'm not sure," said the man.

"Then let's start with your name," I said.

"My name is Pete."

I sensed his crackling nerves on the other end of the line. This wasn't going to be your everyday phone call to a psychic. What it was going to be, I didn't know, but I sensed a lot of pain on his end. A friggin' lot.

"Don't be nervous," I said, and was not very surprised when the big seagull landed on my balcony wall. The big bird was missing a leg, but did a fine job of balancing on just one. How in the hell a seagull could lose an entire leg was beyond me.

No, not beyond me. Not these days. Just as I speculated on the leg, I saw an image of a young man holding what appeared to be a BB gun. The projectile went through the seagull's leg, breaking it and nearly severing it. Nearly. The poor guy had spent weeks in agony until he'd finally chewed off his own leg with his beak.

The animal kingdom endures horrors that few of us could fathom, I had once read. I believe it.

"Well, how much information do I give you, and how much information do I, you know, wait to receive?" he asked.

"We can do this any way you want."

"Well, I would prefer not to say much."

"To test me?"

"Yes, sorry. But it's the only way I can know if you are legit."

"Fair enough," I said. The truth was, I would do the same. His only ace in the hole was that he hadn't told me anything yet, other than his name. "Give me a moment."

I really didn't need a moment. I was already linked into the guy pretty well. But sometimes, it took a moment to make sense of what I was seeing, feeling and hearing. And yes, I experienced all three. A true rarity for a psychic.

Then again, most psychics weren't a source of blood for vampires. Especially powerful vampires. And my very good friend might have been just one of the most powerful vampires ever, although she didn't quite believe it yet.

As I made sense of what I was seeing, as a sort of story unfolded before me, two things happened: the first was that the seagull hopped a little closer on one leg and cocked its head a little to stare at me, and the second was that I gasped.

"You're looking for the person who murdered your daughter," I said to my caller.

There was a long pause. A very long pause. Before sound ripped into my ears. And I suddenly realized that what I was hearing on the other end was the sound of the man sobbing.

CHAPTER TWO

I waited for him to regain control of himself.

While I waited, I reached out further, expanding my mind, but I wasn't God. I didn't know all, see all. I was also not a medium. I didn't see the dead or talk to the dead. I did, however, have other gifts, many other gifts. One of them was remote viewing, which happened to be my strength.

In my mind's eye, I saw a man sitting on a couch in the dark in a living room. The shades were drawn and no lights were on. His phone was pushed up against his ear as he sort of hugged himself in an upright fetal position.

I expanded further out. It was a big home. Nice furniture. A robust leather couch banked one wall. Elegant glass tables reflected light. Framed photos were arranged across the top of a slick, black lacquer piano. I shifted my focus to the photos.

The photos mostly consisted of the man who was now presently huddled on the couch, and also featured an unnaturally blond wife and a naturally blond girl. The girl might have been the cutest thing I'd ever seen. Dozens of pictures lined the piano, and the nearby fireplace mantel, too. I quickly glanced at all of them. The girl sitting at this very piano, the girl in soccer and softball. The girl clowning around with her dad and mom. The girl who ripped his heart with unspeakable agony.

One of the frames said *Penny* on it.

"Was your daughter named Penny?" I finally asked.

He quit crying immediately, gasped. "Jesus. How did you know?"

"You called The Psychic Hotline, remember?"

In my mind's eye, I could see the man desperately wiping away his tears and nodding. He sat up straight.

"You are married." No, wait. That didn't feel right. I got psychic 'hits.' Strong impulses. Strong feelings. This didn't feel right. "You *were* married," I corrected. "To the fake blond. Oops, sorry. Didn't mean to say that. Anyway, you *were* married to the blond in the photographs along your piano and fireplace mantel."

"Jesus."

I waited for more information to come through. It always came through in a variety of ways. With Peter, the information was coming through in feelings, too. Sometimes it came through in symbolic images. Or, if I was getting a particularly clear remote viewing hit, I could just have a look around the tangible environment. I was doing that now, combining my *seeing* with *feeling*.

Yeah, I was weird like that.

But I wasn't getting a hit on the daughter. No surprise there. Not being a medium, I couldn't see or feel the dead. Also, I wasn't a mind reader, so I wasn't privy to what Peter was thinking or what he knew. I got impulses of information. Also, I could not control how much information came through, or what kind of information was revealed. I simply opened myself up to the information…and hoped for the best.

Peter stood and wiped the tears from his face. I saw him pacing in his big living room. I even saw his footprints forming and reforming in the elegant white carpet. He ran his fingers through his hair with his free hand.

As he did so, I began getting more hits, this time flashing images. Horrific images, and as I received them, I spoke with rising alarm. "Your daughter was killed. Strangled to death. She was found in a park nearby. Jesus. Local kids found her. The police don't have a suspect. This was years ago. Maybe two or three years ago. Your wife has long since left you. I'm so sorry. *Jesus.*"

I saw him bury his face in his hands as he sobbed even harder than before.

"You still wear your wedding ring," I said.

As I sat in my cozy chair in my living room, with my protein drink next to me and my eyes closed, I saw him look down at his hand and study the diamond-encrusted band. "How...how could you possibly know that?"

"My strength lies in remote viewing," I said.

"I'm not following..."

"It means I'm watching you now."

He shivered so much he nearly dropped the phone. He began turning in circles, looking around in a panic. As he did so, which I reported seeing, he next went to the front door and looked out, which I also reported seeing.

"That's incredible," he said. "You see my every move."

"My boyfriends all hate it," I said.

"Have you always been like this?"

I thought of my vampire friend. "It's been getting stronger lately."

"What am I doing now?"

I laughed. "You just touched your nose."

"Are you looking into my house somehow?"

"That's one way of putting it, but not in the way you're suggesting."

He sat heavily on the big couch. "I guess you know I just sat down."

"Yes."

"I think I called the right person to help find my daughter's murderer."

"Maybe," I said. "I can't guarantee anything."

"What does that mean?"

"It means I can't control my psychic hits. You do realize, Peter, that most of my clients are lonely women wondering if they'll ever find true love."

I saw him nod. "Yes. I can't imagine you get very many calls like mine."

"No."

"So, what do we do next? I need to know who killed my daughter. I have to know. He has to be found. It's killing me inside."

It wasn't ethical for me to meet a client outside of work. I was not running my own business here. I worked for The Psychic Hotline. My bosses could be listening. Actually, I had a strong sense that they were *not* listening. Not this time.

I bit my lip, thought hard about it. As I thought about it, the one-legged bird continued watching me. I believed in animal totems. My animal totem was a hawk. In some states, seagulls were called sea hawks. If a one-legged seagull could make the journey to see me, I figured the least I could do was make the journey to see Peter.

Finally, I said, "I'm going to need to get to know your daughter a little better."

"What do you mean?"

"I'll need to see her things, touch her things. That kind of stuff."

Now he was nodding enthusiastically, wiping his red nose. "Yes, definitely. Should I give you the address?"

"No," I said. "I'm good."

He laughed a little, even as he wiped the tears. "When can I expect you?"

"Tonight," I said. "Around eight."

"Thank you," he said. "I'll see you tonight at eight." He hung up.

He might have hung up in the physical sense, but he and I were still very much in contact in the psychic sense. I watched him toss aside his house phone, sit back on his couch and cover his face with both hands. One thing I knew above all else, Peter was not his daughter's killer.

I pulled back until I was outside his regal home, and noted the street name and street number. I swung further out and returned to the park I'd seen, the park where his daughter had been found dead. I noted its cross streets. Yes, I was a living, breathing Google Map App. A psychic one.

Such a freak, I thought.

I opened my eyes and gave myself a few seconds to fully return to my small, but cute, apartment in Beverly Hills. I wrote down the street names and address on a pad of paper next to me.

After sipping my protein drink and clearing my thoughts, I took my next call.

"Hi, this is Allison. Thank you for calling The Psychic Hotline. How can I help *you* see into the future?"

CHAPTER THREE

Later, I pulled up to the park.
Yes, the very same park I had seen in my mind's eye when talking to Peter. I was freaky like that. Especially these days, thanks to my friend, Samantha, and before her, Victor. That they were both vampires was no coincidence.

I sat in my car, feeling a deep sadness that I knew was not my own. It was dusk, and the park was mostly empty. A young woman watched two kids swinging. She was looking down at something glowing. It was too big to be a phone. It just might have been one of those Kindle or Nook thingies. Whatever it was, its ambient glow highlighted her lower face and eyes, touching on cheekbones, the tip of her nose, her chin. She highlighted well. The two kids swung and shouted and laughed. The woman ignored them and read, although she glanced up every few minutes.

The park was exactly as I had seen it in my mind. Back in the day, before I had met Victor, a man I would love, a man I would eventually move in with, a man who I would watch die—a man who was, in fact, not a man at all—I had little psychic ability. I would get flashes of insight here and there. Maybe an odd picture would appear in my thoughts. Enough to believe that I certainly had some semblance of a gift. But it wasn't until I'd met Victor—a creature of the night who had fed from me for months—that my psychic abilities had truly awakened.

And boy, had they.

The more that Victor had fed on me, the more my psychic abilities had developed. The brief flashes had turned into longer movies. The hints of knowing had become full-blown facts. It was the most complicated relationship I had ever had, and the most addictive. When I didn't have it anymore, with Victor, I was lost.

And then, I'd met Samantha.

Samantha Moon, my newest friend, was also a bona fide card-carrying member of the nocturnal blood-drinking club. With each partaking of my blood, with each vampire feeding, my psychic abilities continued to expand.

And I was back to the exhilaration of a blood connection with a vampire, one that helped me grow my psychic powers. It was symbiotic, it was beautiful, and it was the most intensely thrilling experience of my life.

I didn't pretend to understand it, but I believed a sort of transference was going on. As in, a part of her transferred to me with each feeding. A part that understood the intangible mysteries of thought and emotion, but one that connected to a tangible reality.

Now, my abilities were primarily remote viewing, with a chaser of clairsentience and clairvoyance. Both of these abilities were still in their infancy, although clairsentience—or the ability to psychically *feel* my way through a situation—seemed to be pulling away. There may have been—*may have been*—some latent pyrokinesis going on as well. That was the ability to start fires. I wasn't sure about this last one, but there had been a moment with a candle in my bedroom that had still left me scratching my head.

It was dusk, but not full darkness yet. I watched the kids swinging as the mom read and occasionally looked up. I waited. What I waited for could be anything. Psychics couldn't just close their eyes and know all. Yes, we were tuned into the spirit world, and sometimes Spirit, as we called it, would divulge a little information…or a lot. Sometimes, we, as psychics, were not tuned into the right frequency, or not searching in the right places. Not open to the bigger answers. Not *ready* for the bigger answers. I suspected our lack of all-knowing was more of a result of not truly understanding our psychic gifts, or ourselves.

Every day, I learned something new. Yes, it would be easier, especially in a criminal investigation, if psychics had access to all knowledge. But we didn't. We saw what we saw. We felt what we felt. We were given what we were given. And hopefully, it all made sense.

But nothing came to me in the park and so, before someone got nervous and called the cops, I started up my Honda Accord and continued along the quiet tree-lined street. As I drove, I was fairly certain I had seen this street somewhere else. Perhaps in a dream. Perhaps on TV.

I didn't know, but there was something compelling about this street.

Something that awakened my psychic knowing.

I thought about that as I drove out to Peter Laurie's residence.

CHAPTER FOUR

Peter greeted me with a smile.
It wasn't a real smile. It was forced. Tight. I suspected the man hadn't smiled a real smile in over two years. The exact moment he realized his daughter was missing had ended his ability to smile. Still, he was quite a handsome man, but I already knew that. Seeing him in person, though, was another story. I found my pulse beating a little faster, until I reminded myself that this man had been through hell—and was *still* going through hell. Which was why I was here. To, apparently, fetch him from the gates of hell and bring him back.

All in a day's work.

He led me inside a wonderfully ornate home filled with original statues tucked in corners and in special nooks, original paintings on the wall, and a lot of old, beautiful furniture. I had a very strong hit, and, like I usually did, I voiced it without thinking: "You inherited the house from your mother."

"Yes, very good. She died a few years ago."

I went over to one of the paintings...a beautiful example of impressionism. They all were. The painter's preferred subject matter was ballet dancers. Same with the sculptures.

"Your mother created these as well."

"You're good, Allison."

"I'm just being me," I said, and walked around one such bronze sculpture that was a thing of beauty. The dancer was pirouetting on her pointed toes, arms circled overhead in mid-spin.

"My brothers and sister have claimed some of them, but for now, they will stay here. At least, until the house sells."

I nodded. I wasn't a medium and I couldn't see the dead, not yet anyway, but I had a very strong feeling that his mother was with us now—and perhaps, even his daughter. Then again, what did I know?

"You're selling the house?"

"Yes. It's time I moved on. I don't want to, but I guess I have to."

An odd choice of words, to be sure. I changed the subject and said, "You love your mother."

"Very much so, and I love her art, too. It's gaining traction. More and more dealers are contacting me and my family. Luckily, she painted a lot. We have hundreds of paintings and sculptures up in her studio, too."

Peter led me through the beautiful home, holding his stomach oddly as we walked, and soon, we stepped under an archway and into another room full of only bronze sculptures on plinths and pedestals. It could have been a collection in a museum. I sensed a presence nearby; that is, if only my skin was any indication. Indeed, the moment I had stepped into the big house, I'd sensed spirit activity. How many there were, I didn't know, but I could feel them, perhaps a few of them, watching me.

Admittedly, this had never happened before. Not to me. As we crossed the sculpture room and into a less formal family room, I paused at the doorway and looked behind me. I was certain I was about to see my first ghost. Or ghosts. The hair on my neck and arms—hell, everywhere—was standing on end. But as I turned, there was nothing there. Nothing that I could see, anyway.

Peter waited for me in the family room.

That I was acting odd in his home didn't seem to faze him. When I was done acting like the nut-job that I was, he gave me a sad smile and motioned for me to sit in the overstuffed couch along one wall. It was the same couch I'd seen him sitting on earlier.

I sat as directed, and he did the same in a matching overstuffed recliner. He still held his stomach. A big fireplace was to my right. That would be fireplace number two. A thick, white, faux polar bear rug spread between us. It was probably heaven for toes. In fact, I itched to take my shoes off and let my toes revel in the fluffiness, but refrained. It wouldn't be ladylike, and Peter Laurie was very much the gentleman.

A TV was opposite the fireplace. I noted an Xbox on a shelf next to the TV. The Xbox was covered in dust. That hit me hard for some reason.

Everywhere were pictures of a beautiful blond woman and a precocious little girl. Yes, something very lost haunted this home, and it wasn't necessarily his deceased mother or their little girl. No, it was Peter himself. Still, I saw a small light in his eyes. The light of hope. Perhaps I was his last hope. No pressure there or anything.

"Would you like something to drink, Allison?" he asked. Although his voice didn't have much inflection, he was still quite the gentleman. I detected the hint of a New England accent. I told him no thank you, and added, "Drinking clouds my connection. So does too much caffeine."

"Then I won't offer you that hot toddy today."

"Say that three times," I said. "But maybe next time." I hoped it didn't sound too flirtatious. I quickly added, "I've never taken on a client outside of work. It's frowned upon."

"Which is why I will make a sizable donation to the charity of your choice. If you're not collecting the money for yourself, perhaps your employers would be forgiving."

"Perhaps," I said. Truth was, I could have used the money, too, but oh well. I knew I would eventually tell my boss about meeting Peter. In essence, ratting myself out. It was a pain in the ass being me sometimes. Although honorable to a fault, I could keep a secret. Just ask my vampire friends.

"Perhaps you should consider opening your own psychic business," said Peter in a voice I was beginning to appreciate as very refined and cultured.

I laughed that off lightly. More truth: I was a big chicken. I liked the stability of working for the Psychic Hotline. I got a steady check. The money was nice. It afforded me to live the life I lived. Living in Beverly Hills was not cheap. Hell, living anywhere in southern California was not cheap. My problem was, of course, that I loved living in Beverly Hills. I loved the restaurants and shops and the people I met.

Beverly Hills had an inimitable creative energy. On any given day, I could run across Michael Bublé or my local TV anchorman. I'd seen everyone from Brad Pitt to Cher. And it wasn't just the stars, either. There was vitality here. Possibilities. A sense of abundance and peace, and I responded well to that. Oh, and did I mention the shopping?

He gave me a small smile. "Just think about it. I think you would be quite good at it, and help a lot of people."

"Now, who is the psychic one here?" I said.

"Certainly not me. I'm just a businessman, and you provide a service that could help a lot of people. Please, just think about it. You'd expand your opportunities and reach so many people who…need you."

"You've barely met me, Mr. Laurie."

"One doesn't have to be in your presence long to know that you are…different—a good different." And now, he really did laugh. A high sound that didn't seem natural. I suspected it was because he hadn't laughed much, if at all, over the past two years, almost three.

"Okay, now that we've established that I'm a big weirdo," I said, winking, "perhaps we should get down to business. But first, let me ask, is there something wrong with your stomach?"

He'd still been holding it and rubbing it absently. The brief merriment was gone. His handsome features drew down, his smile absorbed by his pain. His short hair, I noted, was a good deal grayer now than it had been in many of these photos. He looked down, and said, "Sorry. I ate something bad recently. Stomach's been bothering me ever since."

"Maybe you should take something for it."

"Maybe," he said, and gave me a forced half smile. Yes, he was in some pain.

"Of course," he said. "Where shall we begin?"

"Let's start with your wife," I said. "Why did she kill herself?"

CHAPTER FIVE

Peter stared at me.
He didn't ask how I knew. He didn't mention that I could have found out this information with just a little bit of background work. He just stared at me with rapidly watering eyes.

Finally, he nodded and said, "She was heartbroken."

I felt more tingling and a sadness so great that I hunched over a little, tried to shake it off.

"You see, she was never the same after Penny's murder. Especially considering…"

"Considering what?"

"Well, the two of them had a big fight that morning. Lots of arguing. Penny wanted to wear lip gloss and she was kind of young to start all of that, so Isabelle vetoed it. Then Penny told her mother that she hated her. Isabelle let our daughter's words get to her, and had taken her to school without the two of them making up. She never had a chance to reconcile, you know, and it tore her up."

"That must have been hard."

Peter looked at me. "You have no idea. Yes, she put on a brave face. Even organized a charity in Penny's name and to help other parents of murdered children. But at home, away from the support of the people who organized walkathons and spread the message across social media, Isabelle was lost."

I felt that sense of "lost" and loss, so much so now that I suspected his wife was nearby. Never before had I sensed the departed. Not like this. Hell, my skin was tingling with static electricity. Then again, my powers had continued to grow, and hadn't my vampire friend fed from me just the night before? *She had.* We had had drinks at The Ivy. We had seen Tom Cruise and his daughter having dinner. So had everyone else. God, I would hate to be a celebrity.

Afterward, back at my apartment, after chatting and drinking more wine, I had rolled up my sleeve, sat back on my own couch and closed my eyes as my new friend had drawn her sharpened nail over a vein in my wrist. Yes, the pain had been intense. At first. I always gasped, and last night was no different.

My friend didn't sink her teeth into me. In fact, my friend and I had joked about the TV vampires with their elongated teeth. Vampires, as far as I knew—and my friend would be an expert—didn't have elongated teeth. Why would they? It wasn't very hard for such a powerful creature to puncture the skin and drink, especially with those freakish nails they had.

Anyway, I had sat back and relished the sensation of my friend drinking from my wrist. She never liked me looking at her while she fed, and I didn't blame her. She was a mom, after all. A respected private eye and one-time federal agent. She didn't want to be seen as a monster. Again, I didn't blame her. But, of course, she *was* a monster. A beautiful monster.

Our bloodletting sessions were not sexual. Not like my sessions with Victor. No, Sam and I were friends only, and, well, we didn't swing that way. With that established, our bond was pretty tight. So tight that she and I had almost instantly become telepathically bonded. The bond was growing stronger, too. Sometimes, I caught whiffs of her thoughts from great distances. Up close was different. Up close, we might as well be in each other's minds.

Yes, last night had been another bloodletting. Samantha Moon had drunk deeply from me, so much so that I'd actually felt weak. The wound on my wrist had healed instantly, as soon as she'd pulled away. Sam had looked away shyly, as she always did, her face delicately flushed, my blood on her lips. She never licked her lips in front of me. She always turned away to do that. My friend was an adorable monster. And a fastidious feeder. She never left my apartment looking like a crime scene. I appreciated that.

So, it was of no great surprise that I was certain I could feel his wife's pain. Certain, because I knew she was in the room with us now.

"Your wife's name was Isabelle," I said.

Peter nodded and calmly wiped his eyes. It was late evening and the big house was quiet. Correction, not quite. I heard the old place settling, creaking here and there. Nothing supernatural. At least, I didn't think so.

"I feel her sadness," I said.

He kept nodding and kept wiping his eyes. Except he wasn't able to stay on top of the wiping, and tears spilled down his cheeks.

My skin prickled. I felt cold. I wasn't good enough at this yet to slip inside her thoughts, to hear her, or even to pick up any symbolism she might be using to reach me. I just heard her name, and felt her sadness.

"I'm not a medium," I said. "I'm not very good at this, but your wife is here with us now and she is very, very sad."

I could have made up all of this. Her name would have been easy enough to find. Telling him his wife was here would have been easy enough to say. Except...

"You know she's here, don't you?" I asked.

He nodded and finally gave up wiping his tears. His startling blue eyes were now red-rimmed. "I've seen her, standing behind you over by the fireplace. I've seen her twice. I...I thought I was going crazy."

"You're not going crazy," I said. "We are not alone."

He nodded, took in some air, excused himself politely, and left the room. I heard him creak through the big home and shut himself into another room. What came next I would remember for the rest of my life. Deep, wracking, shuddering sobs radiated through the entire house and seemed to come up through the floorboards themselves. Up through my feet and legs, they completely took hold of me.

But the sobs lasted for only twenty or thirty seconds. Just as quickly as they had started, they stopped. I heard water running, and a few minutes after that, Peter appeared at the arched doorway. That the man had just produced some the loudest, most gut-wrenching sounds I'd ever heard, one would never guess. He looked calm...although mostly, he looked empty.

He said, "I can show you Penny's room now, if you'd like."

CHAPTER SIX

He led me up a spiral staircase. It was my first spiral staircase. I somehow managed to hide my excitement; after all, saying "Whee!" at a time like this didn't seem appropriate.

The stairs led to an upstairs covered with dark mahogany walls and deeply cushioned floors. Once again, I just wanted to take off my shoes and run up and down the hallway on the plush carpeting, which, I suspected, little Penny had done often.

Although I felt an elder and younger presence in the house, neither Peter's mother nor daughter had come through. Not the way Isabelle, his wife, had.

Peter led me down the hallway and past a few generations of family portraits. I had a sense of old money. A sense of his family doing some great things…and not so great things, too. Someone in his family tree had been a shyster who'd ripped people off. Or maybe I was misinterpreting my feelings. It was easy to do sometimes.

Either way, I got good vibes from Peter himself. I hadn't asked what he did for a living, and I didn't look into it, but I saw money around him. I saw stacks of money, and I suspected he was in banking. Very high up in banking, too. My guess would be a vice president of a big bank. The family business, I suspected, was banking.

As I walked past a particularly old portrait, of a man who stared down with snake-like eyes at the camera, and wearing a bowler hat, I knew that not all of the Lauries were good people. I shivered as I walked past the picture.

Down the long hallway—and past an enormous study with a leather-tooled surfaced desk and a chair fit for a king—or at least a vice president of a bank—we soon came upon a row of bedrooms. Six to be exact. Damn big house, although not as big as that island resort I'd had the displeasure of nearly dying in. Or, rather, of being possessed in.

But that was another story.

At one such door, Peter stopped, looked at the handle for a heartbeat or two, then reached for it, turned it and pushed open the door. It swung open silently enough, only squeaking when it reached the end of its arc.

"This was Penny's room," he said, stepping aside and allowing me to enter ahead of him.

As I did so, I got a psychic hit, or a *knowing*, as I called it. "You don't come in here very often."

"Only a few times, and not for a long time," he said behind me. Peter no longer seemed surprised by my *knowings*; at least, he didn't question them anymore.

The room was enormous, and dusty. I suspected that Peter had instructed even the maids to stay away. As I stepped into the dark room, he flipped on the lights. Dust motes swirled. I left actual footprints along what had would have been a beautifully polished hickory floor.

The room was a typical girl's room...a little rich girl's room, actually. There were posters on the wall: cartoon characters, Justin Bieber looking quite young and intense, and horses. Lots of horses. The poster closest to me was slightly faded along its edges. Rust from the thumbtacks had stained the corners a little. In the center of the room was a small bed for a small girl, with lots and lots of floor space around it. A big rug covered some of it and I had an image of a little girl playing with her dolls and reading and even talking on a cell phone, right here on the floor, on the rug. I even had an image of her sleeping on the rug…with her mom. A sort of campout in upscale sleeping bags that had never been used for outdoor camping, only slumber parties. I kept these impressions to myself.

After all, Peter didn't seem to be holding up very well and, as I stood in the center of the room, soaking it in, absorbing the energies, reading the energies, and, in essence, tuning into another world, another place, hell, even another time, Peter stayed back by the door, looking away, looking down the hallway. Mostly, he looked miserable and like he wished he had never opened her bedroom door and looked inside.

The daughter could have been here, or not. I did sense a younger energy nearby, but it was vague. It could be what some psychics called *residual energy*. In effect, I could be sensing her *past* energy, not her present energy. Not all spirits came back. Not all spirits hung around. Many moved on, and if some of my psychic friends were correct, many were re-born as well, into other bodies, other places, perhaps even other times.

It was, of course, all a big mystery to me. And yet, the mysteries were trickling down to me in dribs and drabs. The more Samantha Moon drank from me, the keener I got as a psychic.

I was becoming quite adept at remote viewing. In fact, I was scarily adept at it, so good that I might as well have been in the room with the other person. But that was only if I was "tuned into" them, like I had been when I had Peter on the phone.

I'd never tuned in to the dead. Hell, I'd never even tried. I didn't know where to begin, truth be known, but I had some ideas.

As Peter continued standing near the doorway, dealing with his hurt and loss as best as he could, I moved through the big room. A busy room, too. Stuffed animals crowded under the window, a dollhouse that was as big as my bathroom stood in one corner, and dressers overflowing with trinkets collected from a short life. But in the corner closest to the bed was something different. A painter's easel.

"Your daughter painted?" I asked.

Peter didn't look into the room, instead he continued looking down the hall. He said, "She...she wanted to be an artist."

I nodded, although he didn't see me nod, and headed over to the corner of the room with the easel. Next to the easel was a stack of her paintings. The girl had been good, and seemed to prefer watercolor. She was talented like her grandmother. I knelt down and flipped through the paintings. They were of dogs, all of them. There was Goofy, Pluto, Doug the talking dog from *Up*, Snoopy, Marmaduke, Astro from *The Jetsons*, and one of Dino from *The Flintstones*, although Dino didn't technically count as a dog. Who was I to argue with the logic of a ten year old?

"I take it you have a dog," I said.

Peter shook his head, still looking away. "Sparky went missing on the same day as Penny."

I didn't know what to say, so I didn't say anything. I doubted words would help, anyway. Peter was long gone, and simple platitudes would have fallen on deaf ears. He needed answers, real answers. Not sympathy.

I continued flipping through the paintings until I found a picture of a small, brown-haired little pooch, with the word "Sparky" on his collar. As I looked at it, I got a flash of the little dog barking hysterically, angrily.

A flash of a little girl getting into a car, and of a man's voice telling her it would be okay. A pleasant voice. A soothing voice.

A flash of the dog jumping in as well.

I got another flash, one that was so horrible that I gasped. *Sweet Jesus*, I thought.

When I had gotten some control of myself, I said, "Would you mind if I took the painting of Sparky home with me?"

"Will it help you find my daughter's killer?"

I looked at the painting again as I heard the pleasant voice telling the girl over and over again that it would be okay, to come on in, *it'll be okay*.

"Yes," I said. "I think it will."

"Then take it," said Peter. "It's yours."

I nodded and carefully pulled it out from behind the others. The paper canvas was thick, and had probably been her grandmother's art supplies. With the painting now tucked under one arm, Peter showed me out of the room. As he led me back down the carpeted hallway, we came across something unexpected.

It was a book sitting in the middle of the hallway.

Right there on the cushioned carpet, in a spot that both Peter and I had recently walked over. There had, of course, been no book lying there, just minutes earlier.

"How odd," said Peter, reaching down. He picked it up and examined it, holding it for me to see. It was an old book but not ancient. My guess, from the 60s or 70s. Maybe earlier. The tattered dust jacket read: *Wiccan: A Way of Life*. "Did you see this book here before?" he asked.

"No."

"It was my mother's."

"She was a witch?" I asked.

"And proud of it." He held up the book, eyebrows raised. "But this has been in storage in the garage. I'm sure of it, with her other books. Truth is, they give me the damn creeps."

And as he said this, more goose bumps appeared on my skin. and not just on my arms, but over my entire body. I was suddenly certain, without a doubt, that this book was meant for me. Whether I wanted it or not remained to be seen. As Peter scratched his head and bit his lip, I came to a decision...a decision that would change my life forever.

"Peter, I think your mother wanted me to have this book."

He tore his eyes off the book and placed them on me. "What?"

"I know, it sounds crazy, but I think your mom wants me to have this book."

Peter shook his head. "When it comes to Mother, nothing is crazy. Trust me." He looked at the book again, looked at me, then shrugged. "Knock yourself out—but I would caution you to be careful. This is nothing to take lightly. I've seen...*things*."

He handed me the book, and as soon as I took the book from him, two things happened simultaneously: one, I shivered nearly uncontrollably, and, two, the ghostly image of a tall and regal woman appeared behind Peter.

She smiled at me, nodded, and disappeared.

CHAPTER SEVEN

Morning couldn't have come soon enough. I'd had a rather strange night, filled with dreams of ghosts and girls, of witches and murder.

Now I was sitting on my couch sipping a cup of coffee, with my laptop where it belonged: on my lap.

On the screen before me was simply a local phone call. The Psychic Hotline portal that I logged onto each day only provided me with the caller's city. Never a name or full phone number. This call, I saw, had originated in nearby Santa Monica.

"Hi, this is Allison. Thank you for calling The Psychic Hotline. How can I help you see into the future?"

"Oh, thank God," said a familiar voice.

"So, how long did it take this time?" I asked.

So, when I heard the familiar voice, it was a pleasant surprise… and a bit of a break. I'd just dealt with a longwinded woman who would rather hear herself talk, than me. Which was fine. I wasn't getting a good read on her, anyway, and was questioning what I was telling her. I hated when that happened.

"Took me nine tries this time," he said. "And cost me fifty bucks to finally get you."

"I'm an expensive date," I said.

"Well, it's as close to a date as I can get. For now."

"Forever," I said, laughing, although I admired his persistence. "You know my rules."

"You don't date clients. Plus, you have to say that because *they* might be listening."

"Well, *they* might fire me. And I happen to like this job."

"You have to say that, too, because *they* might still be listening."

I laughed at that. I was sitting on my couch with my legs crossed under me, sipping on a decaf Americano. If I wasn't drinking a protein drink, I often drank decaf before and during sessions. Caffeinated drinks made my mind race just enough that I couldn't tune into the spiritual. In fact, it was a rare day that I actually did have caffeinated coffee. And when I did, I almost always regretted it. I'd become used to connecting to what I thought of as my higher self. This connection was deeply spiritual, and it allowed for some fantastic results, especially when I was tuning into another person. I suspected that it was my higher self that tuned into others, and then reported its findings to me. Caffeine cut off that connection. Not good.

My sliding glass door was open. A bee had found its way inside and came right over to me. I said howdy, then ignored it completely. When it was done checking out the crazy lady in the headset, it found its way out again.

"They're not listening now," I said.

"You're sure?" he asked.

I checked again how I felt about that, and a certain *knowing* came over me. "I'm pretty sure."

"That's good enough for me. So, what are you wearing, baby?"

I laughed. "Nothing you would be interested in."

"Don't be too sure about that."

"Don't be creepy," I said.

I liked Conn. In fact, I was very intrigued by Conn. I got a very good feeling from him. A warm feeling that I couldn't deny. Conn was also a Scorpio, and I knew that you had to keep Scorpios in check. It was easy—very, very easy—for them to turn something fun and light into something steamy and sexual. It was in their natures. God bless their natures.

"Sorry," he said. "You know I didn't mean anything by it."

I know Conn liked to present small openings, always hoping I would jump into them. I never did, although I admired his persistence. And, again, God bless those randy Scorpios. They kept things interesting.

"Forgiven," I said. "Now, to what do I owe the pleasure of this phone call?"

"Do I have to have a reason to call?" he said. "Perhaps I just need to hear your voice."

"Perhaps you need to get a life."

"I do have a life," said Conn. "I'm just missing one thing."

"A cat?" I asked.

"You," he said after a moment.

I snorted at that. "You are such a goofball, Conn. You've never even met me."

"We can change that, you know. I could meet you tonight for drinks."

"That's not gonna happen."

"Yes, I know," he said.

"I'm sorry."

"It's okay," he said. "If this is the only way I can spend time with my dream girl, then I will accept my lot in life. Better a few minutes a week with you, Allison, than no time at all."

I was touched again by his words. "It's your money," I said after a moment, although my tone was now much softer. "Do what you want with it."

"I am," he said, "and I can think of no greater way to spend it than by spending time with you."

"Geez, Conn, have you always been such a romantic fool?"

He thought about that. Little did he know that I could *see* him thinking about it, that I could see him now sitting in his rather lavish home overlooking the Pacific. That I could see that he was, in fact, everything he claimed to be, and perhaps even more. Never did he mention his money, of which he clearly had a lot. I knew his address, too, and I knew his home inside and out.

Yes, I'd even checked out his attic and under his floorboards. No bodies. He wasn't a creep. He wasn't a sicko. He was just lonely.

Or perhaps, as he claimed, in love with me.

That he was also somewhat handsome made things all the more interesting. Of course, he knew none of this, knew nothing of the snooping I'd performed. And, thank God, he mostly wore clothes when he called me.

We chatted some more, about my day, about me, about anything that came to his mind. He paid, of course, for every minute of it. I suspected he could have talked to me all day, and, for some reason, I didn't mind that. Not one bit.

He was halfway through a story about his dog—a dog I could see sitting by his feet now—when I felt a disturbance. Someone had picked up. One of *them*.

"Thank you for the call, Conn," I said, cutting him off. "I hope I was of service to you today."

After two months, Conn knew the routine. "You were incredibly accurate, Allison. Never in all my life have I ever come across a psychic more accurate than you."

Oh, brother, I thought. One thing Conn was good at doing was pouring it on.

He clicked off and I sat back on my couch, decaf Americano in hand, and smiled.

CHAPTER EIGHT

It was early afternoon, and I was at The Whisper Lounge at The Grove with my friend, Bernice.

And, no, we weren't whispering. Truth was, we rarely whispered. I didn't think we knew *how* to whisper. On second thought, I didn't think they much liked us here at The Whisper Lounge.

Anyway, Bernice Jepson was a fairly new friend of mine. I called her Bernie because it suited her better. She had been my trainer at The Psychic Hotline. As in, I sat in on some of her phone calls and made notes. As I made notes and listened in on a few days of her taking calls from clients, one thing had become rather apparent: Bernie was not a very good psychic.

As in, she rarely, if ever, got anything right. She had made an art out of backing out of her statements, re-wording and charging along by distracting the clients with some new "revelation."

While it was true that Bernie was a bad psychic, she was a great friend. That she was slightly delusional and lived with her head in the clouds made her all the more endearing to me. That she thought she was a *good* psychic would be a nice case study in human psychology, one that I would leave to the experts. Perhaps even a team of experts.

Truth was, I found her hilarious. But not in a way that mocked her. She was genuinely caring. And certainly believed she had special powers.

Maybe I was enabling her, but I didn't have the heart to tell her what I really thought of her psychic powers. Anyway, while the waitress brought over our mango margaritas, or mangoritas, Bernie was just wrapping up a story.

"...so I told him that I saw him living in Florida at the beach."

"He must have liked that," I said.

"He said he burns easily and has to do all he can to stay out of the sun."

"But you saw him living at the beach," I said, "in Florida?"

"Right. Working as a, you know, one of those smartly dressed young men who serve you drinks on the sand..."

"A cabana boy?" I laughed. Loudly. I might have even snorted. Some at The Whisper Lounge looked at us and frowned. On second thought, maybe coming to The Whisper Lounge, with its dark mahogany walls and high back booths, wasn't a good idea.

"Right. A cabana boy. Serving drinks on the beach. Not a care in the world. Living in paradise."

"What does he do now?" I asked, sipping from my drink, and enjoying the hell out of this conversation. Perhaps too much. Yes, I thought I enabled her. Did that make me a bad person?

"He works in radio. Has a nice voice. Sounded familiar, actually."

I nodded and tried not to smile. "Would you say he works his dream job now, maybe?"

"Well, maybe," said Bernie, shrugging her rounded shoulders. "But he's obviously not happy. Why else did he call me?"

"True," I said. "Why did he call you?"

"He said he had a question about his love life, wondering if he would ever find 'the one.'"

"And you told him to quit his radio show and work as a cabana boy in Florida, a man who says he needs to stay out of the sun because he burns easily?"

Bernie shrugged again and finished the rest of her mangorita. "What can I say, Allie?" She had her nickname for me, too. "Spirit works in mysterious ways." She waved until she caught the server's attention. "I'm only the messenger."

"You are something," I said into my own drink. Luckily, she didn't hear me.

"So, what's new with you, Allie Cat?" she asked after placing another drink order with our server, this time requesting that the bartender be a little more generous with the booze.

When the server was gone, I said, "I'm working with a client."

"A client? What kind of client?"

"I met him through the Hotline—"

"We don't meet with clients through the Hotline, Al. You know that. It's against the *rules*." She stressed the word and laughed and hiccupped, and now I laughed, too. One thing was certain: Bernie didn't hold her liquor well.

"I know," I said, still laughing, "but he needed help. More help than I could give him over the phone."

"You could get in trouble for that. I'm being serious. It's frowned upon, taking clients away from the Hotline."

"I'm not taking any money."

"Still, they would rather he spend his money on the phone, with *experienced* psychics. No offense, Al."

"None taken," I said, and stifled a smile.

Bernie truly thought that I wasn't in her league. I was fairly new to the Psychic Hotline game, and she had been doing it for a number of years now.

"Be that as it may," I said, "he wanted to meet me to see if I could help him further."

"You should have asked me to come along, Al. You're new to all of this, you could have, you know, made things worse."

"Luckily," I said, "I don't think I did."

"Luckily," she said, shaking her head in a sort of big-sisterly way. "You newbies think you have all the answers. You should listen to us old-timers."

"You're younger than me," I said.

She waved that off and accepted her new drink from the waitress. "You know what I mean. So, what did this guy need—wait, I know."

"You do?" I asked.

"Of course. Geez, Al...who do you think you're talking to? It's me, Bernice Jepson, Psychic to the Stars."

"Only one star, Bernie," I said, "and it was the neighbor on *Desperate Housewives*."

"But he lived on Wisteria Lane. *Wisteria Lane*, Allie Cat. The most famous lane, like, ever."

"He didn't live on it, he was an actor. And he was only on the show for two episodes—"

"But good enough to have been brought back for that second episode." She shook her head sadly at me. "Anyway, let's get back to your client."

"Please."

"He needed help looking for something," said Bernie.

"Very good," I said. Bernie was always pretty good at getting close to the very big picture, but that's where any psychic skills she had trailed off into fantasy.

She nodded, pleased, and drank a lot from her mangorita. "He lost his car keys."

"No."

"His garage door opener?"

"How the heck would he lose a garage door opener?"

"I don't know. But am I right?"

"No."

"His cat?"

"No."

"Dog?"

I thought about that. In fact, he had indeed lost his dog. "Kind of."

"How do you *kind of* lose your dog?"

"It's complicated," I said.

Bernie drank more of her drink and as she did so, I saw something very, very unusual descend upon her. It was a bright ball of light that seemed to fall out of the ceiling, only to disappear down inside her shirt.

What the hell?

Bernie shivered a little and set down her drink. Although she had been glassy-eyed with alcohol, her eyes now looked clear and lucid. She reached out across the table and took my forearm. Her own were ice-cold to the touch. "Then let me uncomplicate things, child," said Bernie in a voice that seemed raspier than her own, and older, too. "You find the dog and you find your answers."

Bernice held my gaze, looking deeper into me than she'd ever had before. Then she released my hand, sat back and shivered.

The ball of light reappeared, hovered briefly, and then faded away.

Bernie immediately reached for her drink.

"Did he lose his car keys?" she asked again.

"You already asked that," I said, still shaken.

"I did?"

"Yes."

"Weird, yeah, I do remember asking that a few minutes ago. Sheesh, this mangorita is hitting me hard."

"That's probably it," I said, and chewed on my lip—a bad habit—and thought about the missing dog, the murdered girl and my goofy friend being briefly possessed.

My life was weird.

CHAPTER NINE

I was sitting in my Spirit Chair, as I called it.
It was a big, comfy recliner with padded arms, padded headrest, and well, padded everything. I read here. I meditated here. I tuned into the spirit world here. This was *my* spot, my place, my escape from the world. No one sat here but me. My phone was turned off. Hell, even my bedroom door was locked symbolically, even though I was the only one who lived in my apartment.

Next to the chair were my favorite spiritual books piled on a small table. Behind the table was a short bookcase filled with even more books. Also on the table was a CD player for meditation CDs, a dowsing amulet tucked away in a black velvet pouch, and a pen and pad of paper for random notes to myself. Yes, I love my dowsing amulet…my direct link into the spirit world.

Then again, I could just be crazy as a bat. If anyone asked my mom, she would vote for crazy. My mom was quite religious and thought anything that "tuned in" to the spirit world was a device intended to confuse us, and allowed the Devil's minions access to our thoughts and world.

I thought my mom was cute, and appreciated her concern.
But I had other ideas.
Now, I wasn't meditating or dowsing or reading. I was sitting here in my overstuffed chair with the watercolor painting of Sparky spread over my lap, my legs crossed beneath me, wearing my biggest, fluffiest socks.

So far, I wasn't getting anything. Not even a tingling. I hated it when that happened. Nothing.

Wherever little Penny was, she wasn't with me now. And how to access her, or the energy within this painting or who the devil killed her, was still beyond me.

Maybe Bernie was right. Maybe I was doing more harm than good. And hadn't Bernie also said, "Find the dog, and you will find your answers."

Except, of course, I was fairly certain that wasn't Bernie speaking.

I sighed, set the painting aside, and reached for the book on Wicca...

CHAPTER TEN

Three hours later, I closed the book.
Okay, *that* was an experience. That was also fairly life-changing, although I still wasn't sure what to make of what I had just read.

Pagans and spells and rituals and sex—sweet mama, all the sex!

Wicca was an Earth-based religion…and one that did not seek out converts. You found your way to Wicca, one way or another.

I thought of the book appearing in the hallway, and snorted. It may not seek out converts, but it sure as hell had a funny way of finding me.

I drummed my fingers on the hardback book.

Seriously, what had I just read?

And was it something I was willing to look deeper into?

I had been raised Catholic. Witches were considered evil, Satan's spawn. I never believed they were, of course, although I was certainly aware that some of us could tap into darker energies…that, in fact, dark energies had tapped into some of us.

I shuddered again at my own recent experience with demonic possession. And to think that my good friend, Samantha Moon, lived with such a possession daily.

Jesus.

It was getting on midnight. The witching hour? I nearly laughed. Did I want a glass of wine? I thought so.

I got up from the Spirit Chair, stretched, and headed into the kitchen, carrying the book with me. As I poured myself a healthy finger or three of wine, my mind was on witches and festivals and Mother Earth, and wondering what the hell was happening to me.

My mind sure as hell wasn't on ghosts.

Except that's what I'm pretty sure just appeared before me, right there in my kitchen.

CHAPTER ELEVEN

I dropped the wine.
The glass promptly shattered, splashing wine everywhere, and sending glittering shards of glass everywhere. *Alcohol abuse*, as my friends in college would say. Anyway, I was pretty sure a shard had lodged into my toe, and I wasn't sure if the red liquid pooling around my bare feet was blood or wine. Probably a little of both.

I continued looking at my feet…yes, there was a sparkly shard right there, lodged into my little toe. *Poor piggie*, I thought, and nearly laughed. I wondered if Samantha Moon would find my bloody toe appealing.

I laughed, because I was sure I was going nuts.

Still, I looked down, unable to look up, to confront what might still be in my kitchen. Correction, what I was certain was still in my kitchen.

Whoever it was, or whatever it was, I could feel it. No, not an it. The same woman from Peter Laurie's house. The same woman who had appeared behind him. She was here, in my kitchen, standing over me. I could feel her compassion, her warmth, her love, her curiosity. Mostly, though, I could feel her determination. Her resolve. For what, I did not know.

I was going to have to eventually look up. I was going to have to eventually confront what, exactly, was in my kitchen. Damn, now the pain in my toe was setting in, too.

I had to do something. I couldn't ignore the blood or the pain…or the ghost.

So, I raised my head slowly, very slowly, afraid to look, afraid of seeing what I knew was still standing there, watching me.

Correction, not standing.

Hovering...as in a few inches off the ground.

As in, I wasn't even entirely sure she had feet.

As in, I was sure I was about to faint, and it certainly wasn't because of the loss of blood. It wasn't that much blood, after all.

It was because I was looking at my very first ghost.

As I braced myself on the kitchen counter, as I forced myself not to stagger and ultimately fall across the floor covered in broken glass, the woman in front of me spoke.

Yes, spoke.

Real words, in real time, for anyone within earshot to hear. "Breathe, dear. You've seen worse."

She was right, of course. I had seen worse. I had felt worse, too. I had seen and lived through what many would consider a nightmare—and just recently, too. That I was still in one piece and not possessed by a demon was more a credit to my friend Samantha Moon keeping her cool than anything I had done. Hell, I had made things worse. But, again, that was another story for another time.

"Deep breaths, dear. Slowly."

"Am I...am I dreaming?"

"No, dear."

She was an old woman, perhaps very old. Like in her nineties and beyond. Yet, she had surprisingly wonderful posture, shoulder back, chin up, back straight, hands folded in front of her... at least, I think they were. Her hands were faded and hazy. Even crazier, she looked familiar. I'd seen her recently, and not just in Peter's house.

"I don't feel very well."

"I don't imagine you do, and I see that you cut yourself. It's a little worse than you think. You need to take care of that, dear."

"How do you—never mind," I said, backing out of the kitchen slowly, bracing myself on the counter. Luckily, the glass smash and spill zone was further into the kitchen, toward the spirit now watching me closely. The spirit that I could see *through*.

With the path behind me relatively free of broken glass, I picked my way slowly, leaving a small trail of blood in my wake. The spirit, mercifully, did not follow. Instead, she watched me closely. At least, I thought she was watching me closely. Truth was, I was doing my best to avoid any kind of eye contact with her.

And when I was off the linoleum and on the carpet, I hopped up on one foot so as not to track blood through it...or, at least, that was the plan.

The reality was far less graceful.

I fainted right there on the carpet.

CHAPTER TWELVE

I awoke in the same spot.

As I lay there blinking, face pressed against the white fibers, briefly wondering where the hell I was, and who I was with and how much I had drunk.

Until I remembered the ghost.

I gasped, but didn't move or even open my eyes. I just lay there, accessing the situation.

I was fairly certain I was alone.

Of course you're alone, an inner voice told me. Perhaps the last remnants of my logical ego. *And ghosts don't exist.*

I nearly laughed at that as I sat up. I'd hit my head pretty hard, carpet or not. How long I was out, I didn't know. A few minutes at least, maybe longer. Gingerly touching my head, I noted that I didn't feel the same electrical, staticy feeling I'd felt when the spirit had manifested.

Definitely too weird for someone sober.

Yes, I still wanted that drink.

First, I hobbled into the bathroom. My toe had quit bleeding on its own, but it needed some doctoring. I did the best I could with my foot up on the sink, cleaning it first with hot water, then applying alcohol and peroxide. The attention to the wound had started the blood moving again, but not by much. Soon, my little piggie was bandaged and ready to face the world.

Ghosts and all.

I limped back into the kitchen and spent the next fifteen minutes sweeping and hunting down glass fragments like the *Inglourious Basterds* hunted down Nazis. Or not. When I had done my best sweeping and eyeballing the shards, I next used a small kitchen vacuum that I kept in a front closet. Now sweating a little, I finally had that glass of wine.

As I poured, I said, "Whoever you are, can you please wait until I'm sitting before scaring the unholy shit out of me?"

I waited for a response, didn't get one—which relieved the hell out of me—and made my way into the living room. Once there, I set the glass down on a coaster on the glass coffee table, like a good girl, and, as I reached for the remote with every intention of wasting my night away in front of the TV, watching everything from nerds to half men to country singing contests, I saw something very strange lying by the remote.

It was the Wicca instructional book for beginners. A book that I'd left in my bedroom, by the Spirit Chair.

"Holy hell," I said.

I glanced around my small apartment, hoping like crazy that I wasn't about to see a floating old lady who, I was now fairly certain, was Peter's departed mother.

I drank more wine.

A lot more wine.

Almost all of it.

The book. It was sitting on the arm of my couch, as if I'd just set it there minutes earlier. I hadn't, of course. I'd been out cold on the carpet minutes earlier, and prior to that, I had last seen the book in my bedroom.

Even more curious, I could see that there was something in the book, something I hadn't put there myself.

"Curiouser and curiouser," I said.

I tentatively picked up the book. That something strange and miraculous was happening to me *right now*, I had no doubt. I could feel it. My skin was tingling. The hair on my head and arms bristled. It was as if the room was suddenly filled with a low dose of electricity. Although I was still new to the psychic world, I knew that something bigger than me was happening, happening right now, and that I needed to be strong and power through and, most importantly...

"No more fainting," I whispered to myself.

I opened the worn book carefully, turning to the page with the bookmark. The bookmark consisted of an old receipt of mine. Really, really old. I looked again, blinking. Three years old, in fact. From a car wash in North Hollywood. NoHo, as we called it here. I continued blinking, staring at it. The receipt must have been in an old pair of jeans. Or dropped and forgotten at the back of my closet. Or in an old drawer or even in my car. All I knew was that I sure as hell hadn't seen it in years, and, quite, frankly, I barely remembered going to the car wash.

I was about to wad it up and toss it aside when a flash of memory occurred to me. Yes, I did, in fact, recall going to the car wash. This was back before I had met Victor, the man—or creature—who would first introduce me to the world of vampires.

Three years ago, I had been a personal trainer and somewhat aimless. Yes, I'd always known that I had some psychic skills, and a part of me had always wanted to explore that. But mostly, those thoughts had been in the background, flaring only briefly when I'd get a psychic hit, only to recede again quickly.

But one day, all that had changed, hadn't it?

I nodded to myself. *It had.*

And it had changed at the car wash.

As I looked at the receipt and thought about that day, I gasped and said aloud, "You've gotta be kidding me."

I didn't remember much about the car wash, but I did remember the old woman watching me.

I had been sitting in the waiting area, probably reading a book or a magazine or on my phone texting. I'd just gotten into texting back then, and that had been the death of me. I both loved and loathed texting, as technology was both loved and reviled by me. It put a degree of separation between me and other people, and yet in some ways, like the Psychic Network, it was a tool to bring me close to people with whom I would not otherwise ever connect.

Anyway, I now remembered, more than anything about that day, the overwhelming feeling that someone had been watching me. The feeling was very familiar to what I was feeling now, here in my apartment. A slow, steady, ripple of electrical current. Almost a buzzing in my ears. *Almost.* A sense that eyes were on me, moving over me, penetrating me, looking so deeply that nothing was hidden. Nothing.

I remember shivering and looking up, glancing around…and seeing her sitting across from me. She was alone. And old. Very, very old. So old that I thought someone should be with her. But there was no one. No grandkids, no bored sons or daughters. She was also staring at me. Intently. I smiled. She didn't. I looked away. She didn't. I knew this because when I sneaked a peek back at her, she was still staring at me. I swallowed uncomfortably and shifted and tried to read but I couldn't. After all, *she* was staring at me. *She* was distracting me. *She* was unnerving me.

And that's when a towel boy waved his towel and indicated that my Accord was done. I had leaped up quickly. I tipped the kid, got in, and was about to pull out of the car wash and onto busy Ventura Boulevard when I forced myself to look back…and saw that the old lady was gone.

As if she hadn't ever stood there.

It had been unnerving.

I'd forgotten about it totally.

Until now.

"That was you, wasn't it?" I said to the empty room, still looking at the receipt.

"Of course, dear," said a voice just behind my ear. "Now, can we talk?"

CHAPTER THIRTEEN

I jumped and squealed and nearly peed myself, but just as quickly as the fear and panic gripped me, it subsided, and I was left gasping and catching my breath, one hand clutching my chest. The other, clutching the wine.

"Please," I said after a moment, and after I was sure I had full control over my bladder, "please, never do that again."

As I breathed and held my hand over my chest, knowing that I was either going crazy or was experiencing the mother of all hauntings, I felt the sizzle of an electric current pulse through me. Stronger than before.

Not crazy, I thought. *Option B…a haunting*.

The old woman materialized slowly before me, taking on substance and shape and detail, and had every skeptic in the world been here with me, watching this, they wouldn't be a skeptic anymore. They would be a believer in all things supernatural. And my little apartment would be crowded as hell. Hell, I could charge admission.

"Holy shit," I whispered.

"Please, dear, you're better than that."

It took me a moment to realize that a ghost had just chastised me for swearing.

I didn't apologize. I just closed my mouth and held my breath and listened to the small squeal that was trying to make its way out from my compressed lips, a squeal that very likely would turn into a scream. But I kept it bottled up, somehow.

In a matter of maybe half a minute, a woman who was mostly solid—after all, I could still see my fireplace mantel through her shoulder area—was standing before me, hands folded below her waist, rising and falling gently. She could have been standing in a boat in the middle of a lake. She wasn't, of course. She was standing in my living room.

"Sweet mama," I finally said.

"Hello, Allison," she said.

"Erp," I said. That was supposed to, of course, be a "hi."

The woman was mostly white, which surprised me. Samantha Moon, my vampire friend, had described ghosts as pure energy. I wasn't seeing pure energy. I was seeing something cottony, with splashes of color. Something mostly solid, but also opaque in spots, too. Whatever Samantha had been seeing, she hadn't been seeing what I was seeing now. Then again, vampires were weird.

"I didn't mean to frighten you," said the ghost. Her voice had a slightly musical quality to it and seemed to reach me from everywhere at once. As if her voice was coming out of surround sound speakers.

That's when I realized that her voice wasn't coming from everywhere at once. It was coming from inside my ear. As in, inside my head.

"Sweet Jesus," I whispered.

"He is sweet," said the woman. I watched her lips move, watched her speak, but the words appeared directly in my head. "The name has power, as do many names and words, for that matter. Do not speak it lightly, dear."

"This isn't happening," I said, suddenly sure I was dreaming. I looked around. I wasn't in bed. I was on the couch. I stood suddenly, with the thought of splashing water on my face in the bathroom, but a sharp pain in my foot changed that plan. I gasped and sank back into the couch. The pain in my toe was enough to convince me I wasn't dreaming.

Now breathing hard, I had worked myself up. "I need air," I gasped.

"Then get some air, dear."

I stood and staggered through the room, keeping one eye on the spirit who turned and watched me cross the room and head over to my balcony. There, I threw open the sliding glass door and breathed the not-so-fresh Beverly Hills air. I smelled traces of exhaust, yes, but I also smelled the nearby jacaranda trees, which were blooming, and the freshly cut grass, too. Good enough. I sucked and breathed and repeated, and was certain that by the time I turned around, the old woman who had appeared in my apartment would be gone.

Yes, of course, she would be gone, I thought, looking out toward the massive apartment edifice before me with its glass facade and covered balconies and awnings and doorman. Yes, this was the real world. The physical world. A world where ghosts did not exist. Ghosts would not even be allowed in Beverly Hills, if Beverly Hills had any say in it. Ghosts were something out of... *Hollywood.*

And so, as I turned away from the balcony, I was certain that whatever I had seen—or imagined—would be gone. Samantha and I would have a good laugh over this during drinks later. *Maybe I should see a shrink,* I thought, and, as I turned, I felt the now-familiar buzz on my skin, and there she was, standing there in my living room, rising and falling on the unseen tides of time and space, watching me serenely.

My heart sank...but I was excited, too. "You're Peter's mother," I realized, when I stepped back into the living room from the balcony.

"Yes, dear."

"You gave me the book."

"Of course."

She spoke calmly, patiently, with no inflection in her voice and no gestures, either. She could have been a projected image in my room. Except that her eyes and head followed my movements.

"Why did you give me the book?"

"I sense potential in you," she said. "A lot of potential."

"But you're dead."

"I've never been more alive, child."

"I need to sit down," I said. "Wait. I need more wine."

I got the wine, aware that she was watching me carefully, aware that I was already getting used to the light buzzing of static electricity on my skin.

Soon, I was back on the couch, sitting opposite a ghost who was still standing in my living room. Still drifting and floating and staring at me.

"You are dead, right?" I asked. I'd never sounded crazier in my life.

"I passed on a number of years ago, yes."

"So, how...how are you here now?"

I knew something of ghosts, thanks to all those damn ghost documentaries I'd seen. Ghosts needed to draw on energy to materialize. The buzzing...

"You're drawing on *my* energy," I said.

And now, for the first time, she smiled. Also, for the first time, I saw some color appear on her lips. Faint red lips. I knew what this meant. She was getting stronger, filling out, so to speak. From me.

Which could explain why I was feeling tired.

"Yes, dear. I am drawing on you."

Two things occurred to me: one, did she have a right to draw on my energy without asking? And two, had she just read my mind?

"The answer to both is yes, dear," said the old woman in my living room.

"I'm going to need more wine—"

"Not now, child. I need you fully here, fully aware."

"This isn't happening—"

"It is, dear. Stop doubting yourself, or doubting the state of your mental health. Spirits are real. They're all around you.

Every day. I'm real. I'm here now, before you. You know this to be true."

"Okay, fine. I see you. I hear you. But that doesn't make this right. Or wrong. You're a ghost...and you just read my mind."

"I prefer the term *spirit*."

I nearly laughed. "Was I not being politically correct?"

The spirit's facial expressions didn't alter. I wondered if they could change. Perhaps that was asking too much of her etheric body to perform the more subtle movements.

"You were not being *spiritually* correct, dear," she said, correcting me. "Ghosts are those who have not moved on, those who are stuck on this plane, those who are afraid. Those who are, in general, new souls."

"So, what does that make you?" I asked.

"A very old soul, child, and so are you."

As she spoke, another flash of recognition came over me. Yes, I knew her, but not from the car wash. Not even from this life. In fact, I was suddenly certain I knew the old woman very well from another place and time.

I said, "Hello, Millicent."

Lord, help me.

CHAPTER FOURTEEN

I wanted more wine—a lot more wine, in fact—but, after using the bathroom, I resisted the urge to hang a left into the kitchen and, instead, hung a right back into the living room.

Gone was my hope that the old woman would be gone. I was happy that she had not followed me into the bathroom. I just knew she was still in the house because my skin was still buzzing away, still tingling, still doing its groovy thing to alert me that *here be ghosts*.

And, truth be known, the old lady was right. I *did* want to remember this. All of it, and I needed to know that what I was seeing was *real*, and not some alcohol-induced hallucination. If, of course, there was such a thing, which I doubted.

Most important, I wanted to remember, and, yes, I needed my head to be very clear.

She was still there, of course, hovering, watching, waiting. I was briefly tempted to pull out my phone and take a picture of her, or, even better, to film her. But that would have been stupid. The moment I reached for the phone, I suspected she would disappear, and perhaps never reappear again. I didn't want that. Not now. Not before I knew what the hell was going on, and what she wanted with me.

"You're wondering why I'm here, Allison?" she said as I sat back down on the couch before her.

"The thought crossed my mind. Which you would know, since you can read my thoughts. And since when could spirits read thoughts, anyway?"

She did not answer at first. She continued standing there, floating, her hands clasped together below her waist. For the first time, I noticed she wore a wedding ring.

After a moment, Millicent said, "You gave me permission, dear. Long ago, in another place and time."

"Convenient," I said. "But what if I don't want you in my head?"

"Then ask me to leave."

I drummed my fingers on the couch arm. The couch arm was cushioned, so the drumming was mostly muted. "Why are you here?"

"We have unfinished business, dear."

"Who are you? Who are you *really*?"

"I am many things, honey. I have been many people. As have you, but one thing has remained constant."

She didn't have to explain further, I felt it. I knew it. The electrical tingling morphed into real goose flesh. I shivered. "Friends," I said. "We've always been friends."

"We've been *more* than friends, dear. We've been sisters and daughters and mothers. And, a few times, brothers. Except we didn't like being brothers very much. Boys aren't quite as evolved, you see."

As I stared at her, the words *soul mate* appeared in my thoughts. I suspected Millicent had placed it there.

"Soul mates?" I repeated.

"In a way, yes, although many incorrectly infer that the word applies to a single soul. In fact, you have many soul mates."

"And you are one of them?"

"Yes, dear. A very special one. Myself, and one other."

"One other? A man?"

"Not in this life, no."

"Another woman?"

"Yes."

"Great. I can't buy a break. Who is she?"

"You've met her, dear."

I knew exactly who she talking about. My latest friend. My freaky new friend, in fact. Made sense. Samantha Moon and I had hit it off immediately. From the get-go, she'd felt like the sister I'd never had, even as she drank from me.

I focused on the spirit before me. "Were we, um, ever lovers?"

She shook her head and smiled. I might have actually blushed. That was a new one: blushing while talking to a ghost. "No, dear. Never lovers. Friends and siblings. There is, let's say, another soul group that's reserved for our physical intimacy."

"My head hurts."

"I imagine it does."

"But I didn't know you in this life," I said. "I didn't know you or your son, or your granddaughter." A granddaughter, I knew, who had been murdered.

"Not physically, no."

"Which is why you are coming to me now...like this."

"One of the reasons," she said.

"And what's the other reason?"

"I can instruct you better from the spirit world."

"Instruct me in what?"

She smiled and looked down at the table. At the Wicca instructional manual that was still sitting there, placed there by her, in fact.

"In witchcraft?" I asked.

"In Earth-based magic, dear. I prefer to call it Earth magic."

"I don't understand," I said.

"I'm here to remind you, Allison, of what you really are."

"And what am I?"

"You are, of course, a *witch*."

CHAPTER FIFTEEN

I needed wine. Badly.
So, despite Millicent's earlier admonition—and, last I checked, wasn't she a friggin' ghost?—I got up and poured myself a healthy dose of wine. This was, of course, just far too much for me to deal with without at least a little alcohol. Okay, maybe a lot. Wine calmed me. I loved having it in my hand. I found it comforting. Also, I loved the taste of it.

When I sat back down, Millicent, amazingly, looked different. Younger.

She answered my unspoken question for me. "I wasn't always an old woman, you see."

"Suit yourself." I drank deeply from the wine. I sensed Millicent's disapproval. I ignored her disapproval.

"Are you comfortable, dear?" she asked.

"I am," I said, and held up the wine. "Now that I have this."

"I do not understand the need for inebriation."

"Then you don't understand me."

"I know you very well, dear. And never before have you been so interested in alcohol."

I held up the wineglass again. "Welcome to the new me."

"Very well," she said. "I need to tell you that I'm here for another reason, too."

"Fire away."

She looked down at her mostly solid hands. I could have been wrong, but she seemed to be growing younger and younger with each sip of wine. Mid-fifties now, I'd say.

She said, "I'm here to also help my son."

"Peter?"

"Yes. He's stuck on this tragedy, unable to move on. Unable to deal with the loss of his daughter. He needs answers. He needs help."

I thought about her words, drumming my longish nails against the wineglass. The clicking was peculiarly loud in my little apartment. Something wasn't sitting right with me here, something that I couldn't quite put my finger on.

"That's the wine, dear," said Millicent. "Clouds your thinking."

"Oh, put a cork in it," I said, and laughed at my own pun.

"What's troubling you, dear, is that a part of you thinks that, in spirit, I have all the answers."

I snapped my fingers and pointed at her, nearly spilling my wine in the process. "That's it. You *are* in spirit. You can appear in my home, his home, and God knows where else. For all I know, you can speak directly to Penny herself and ask who the killer was." I was on a roll. "Hell, you could probably speak to God himself. Why do you need me to provide any answers?"

"I must remain at a distance, dear."

"Even so, now a killer walks the streets. A killer you might very well know the identity of?" It might be the wine talking—yes, I'd now drunk about half of the glass—but the idea of Millicent knowing full well who the killer was and keeping this information from her son, who was clearly struggling with his daughter's murder, was appalling to me.

"Do not be too appalled, dear. It is the nature of the physical world you live in."

"What the devil does that mean?"

"It means, that not all answers to all problems are given to you. Or to my son. In the mortal life, you must seek answers."

"But you are here, trying to help him through me."

"I am still his mother, and he is my troubled son."

"Who decides these things?" I asked. I stood deftly, managing not to spill my drink, which was getting easier and easier to do as the contents drew lower to the bottom. "I mean, who decides that you can't help your son? Or, for that matter, why don't spirits help all of us know more? Surely, one of you up there knows where Jimmy Hoffa was buried, or who really shot Kennedy, or who's responsible for every unsolved murder case out there. What gives? Why the secrecy? Why are we left to struggle and writhe and stumble in the dark?"

"You assume I have all the answers, dear."

"I assume you have more answers than me since, well, you're dead or in spirit or whatever the hell you call it. I also assume that you're sticking to some sort of spiritual rule book. I want to know who makes these rules and why?"

I had somehow ended up back in the kitchen and back to the wine bottle, which had mysteriously ended up in my hands. Okay, maybe it wasn't such a mystery. I filled the glass and returned.

She waited for me before speaking again. "We help more than you know, dear. But, yes, we are limited in our help."

"Limited by whom? Or is it *who*? Whatever. Who stops you? And why would they stop you from helping someone?"

"There's helping, dear. And then there's helping *too much*. All help first goes through that soul's higher self, and then through the spirit guides. The higher self and spirit guides decide what is best for the incarnate soul."

I'd heard about higher selves and spirit guides and incarnates and discarnates and reincarnation. But hearing it from a spirit was something else entirely. It made things *real*.

"And the person living has no say in it?" I asked.

"The person living has the *final* say, dear."

"So, why are you here now?" I asked. "Are you sort of circumventing the rules?"

"I'm using whatever leverage I can to help my son."

I thought about that, watching the spirit standing before me. She didn't look much like a spirit now. She looked three-dimensional. She had substance and depth and definition. The more she stood in my room, the more she came to life, so to speak. Although she did continue to rise and fall ever so slightly. Most interesting, she continued to grow younger and younger before my very eyes. If I had to guess, she was now in her early forties. She was now a beautiful, dark-haired woman.

She was a good mom, too, and a good person. I sensed that about her. No, I somehow *knew* that about her. After all, according to her, we had been a type of soul mates throughout time and space.

Life is so very, very weird, I thought.

"So, what do you want me to do about your son?" I finally asked.

"Help him find the answers he needs to move on."

"Except I hardly know what I'm doing."

"The answers will come, dear, if you ask the right questions."

"Fair enough," I said, "and you can quit with that 'dear' crap. You look younger than me now."

She smiled and nodded, and with that, she slowly disappeared before my eyes.

I stared down into the wine, shook my head, and, after a few minutes, said, "Okay, that did *not* just happen."

CHAPTER SIXTEEN

I was at the park again.

It was a rainy April morning, which meant, at least in southern California, this would be the last rain we would see in nine months.

I liked the rain and didn't run from it. In fact, I wasn't even using an umbrella now. Such a rebel. I did, however, have a hoodie on. I wasn't a total idiot and I had spent thirty minutes on my hair earlier this morning.

Such a waste, but that was the price one paid for living and working in Beverly Hills. Twice a week, I worked as a personal trainer at the Beverly Hills Gym. No, not the most ambitious name, but our clients were devoted and wealthy and paid good money for personal trainers. I liked good money.

So, I made it a point to look my best on these days. After all, *I* was my own best advertisement.

I checked my phone. I still had an hour before my first client. He was a big film producer. Actually, he was a small-time film producer, but a big man. Most important, he wasn't a pervert, which I always appreciated.

So, I sat back on a bench that countless mothers had sat on before me, watching their children play in this small neighborhood park, complete with jungle gym and swings. Had this been any other day, kids would have been here, I'm sure, and mothers and fathers and grandparents. Their kids would have been dressed in designer clothes with designer shoes. This was, after all, Beverly Hills. And, being Beverly Hills, there would have been a fair share of nannies out here as well.

I was a new psychic. I had one extraordinary skill—remote viewing—a skill that did little good now. My other skills were still blossoming rapidly. I still didn't know what to do for Peter.

Millicent had said to ask the right questions. So, what were the right questions? I knew an obvious one...

"Who killed you, Penny?" I asked.

A name didn't appear in my thoughts. Nor did I hear it whispered in my ear, or on the wind, but was feeling...something. A tingling.

"Penny?" I asked.

I closed my eyes and listened to the rain drum along the concrete path nearby, listened to it slap the leaves above me. The same electrical buzz was alive on my skin, a buzz that I now knew meant the dead were near.

"Penny," I whispered again, and now, I saw her in my mind's eye. I saw her standing nearby, watching me. But the image quickly morphed into her painting of her dog, Sparky.

Penny didn't make a full appearance, not like her grandmother. But I felt her nearby, watching me. Perhaps it wasn't really her. Perhaps it was just an *imprint* of her. I wasn't a medium, and unless a spirit made actual physical contact with me, I was having a devil of a time connecting with her.

I sighed. She was near. I could feel her.

"Who hurt you, Penny?" I asked. "Who?"

"I ask the same questions," said a voice from behind me. "But, admittedly, I'm usually weeping when I ask them."

I gasped and spun around. I knew the voice. It was Peter, standing behind me, drenched to the bone. He was wearing a suit and tie and his shiny shoes. I hadn't heard him approach, thanks to the drumming rain and dripping water.

"I'm sorry," he said. "I wasn't sure who was sitting here, and by the time I saw it was you, I realized I might frighten you anyway."

"No, it's okay," I said, although my rapidly beating heart told me it was anything but okay. Jesus H. Christ, the man nearly gave me a heart attack. "I'm a psychic, I should have known you were standing there," I said, laughing lightly.

"You were trying to make contact with her," he said. It wasn't a question.

"Yes. Except I really don't know what I'm doing."

"Neither do I," he said. "Do you mind if I sit?"

"No, please do."

I scooted over and he came around and sat on the other end of the bench. The rain had, if anything, increased. Peter didn't seem to mind. I watched as water dripped steadily from the tip of his nose. He looked lost, helpless, forlorn.

"I miss her so much," he said. "Both of them."

I nodded, watched a car drive by slowly, probably staring at the two loonies sitting in the rain.

"Do you…feel her at all?" he asked. "My daughter?"

"I do," I said. "Or I thought I did."

"Could you see her?"

"No, not yet. Although I saw her painting in her bedroom. But I suspect that's just an imprint of her, a sort of scene replaying itself over and over in your house."

A faint smile touched his lips. He looked past me, took a deep breath. "I would do anything to see her again."

Ask the right questions…

"When was the last time you saw your daughter alive, Peter?"

"When she left for school that morning."

"Who was the last person to see her alive? I'm sorry if these questions are hard."

"No problem. I've answered them a million times, to the police, reporters and the private eye we hired."

"And no one turned up anything?"

"We've turned up some things, but not enough to catch her killer. You should talk to a Detective Smithy over at the Beverly Hills station. The case is still open, of course, although I haven't spoken to him about it in over a year. He knows everything. I'll ask him to see you."

I made a mental note of the name and we sat there together some more, in the rain, until I had to leave for my training appointment.

By the time I made it back to my car, started it, and looked back, Peter was gone. I cried into my hands, feeling his sadness, and then purging his sadness through my own tears.

It took me a while to get a hold on my emotions and when I finally did, I began to understand why the spirits couldn't just hand us answers to life's hard questions. We were obviously meant to seek answers and by doing so, raise *new* questions.

I drove off, more determined than ever to find Penny's killer.

CHAPTER SEVENTEEN

After my training session, and after I had showered and changed at the gym, I headed straight to the Beverly Hills Police Department.

This wasn't my first time here. I'd been brought in for questioning on the night my vampire boyfriend had been found with a silver arrow in his chest. The police wanted answers and grilled me relentlessly about my murdered boyfriend. I told them I hadn't a clue who'd broken into the house, or why my boyfriend had been shot in his sleep, with an arrow, no less. Or why the man had spared me.

Truth was, the man had nearly sent an arrow into my own chest, too. Never had I been so afraid, or so devastated. The vampire hunter had shown some compassion towards me, and listed a handful of murders around Los Angeles that my now-dead boyfriend, whose blood was even then pooling in the bed next to me, had committed. I didn't doubt the hunter. I knew my boyfriend was a killer. But I was addicted to him. Or, more accurately, addicted to him *feeding* from me.

Few knew that a vampire's victim derived just as much pleasure from the feeding as did the vampire himself. And I derived much, much pleasure. More importantly, with each feeding, I could feel my psychic powers increasing, sharpening.

Anyway, I had been hauled down here for questioning, twice. The police had been baffled over my boyfriend's murder. They were certain I had something to do with it. I had been a go-go dancer before meeting Victor. For two months, I'd lived well. No, I'd lived like a queen. A true whirlwind romance of lovemaking, feeding and shopping. Honestly, what more could a girl want?

But I kept to my story: a break-in, I'd awakened to find Victor gasping, and a man standing in the doorway holding a crossbow. Those were the facts. I neglected to mention a few *additional* facts. That Victor was a vampire, that he had killed often, and that he was getting his just due by a vampire hunter.

Just or not, his murder tore me up for a long, long time. I had literally been addicted to him, to the feeding, to the lifestyle, even to what I thought had been love.

The police, of course, didn't like it, but in the end, my story held up purely through forensic evidence. Ample evidence of a break-in, and a murder weapon that I had no association with. That I could have staged the break-in with another, to rob my boyfriend, was a possibility they had brought up. I reminded them that I was already living with Victor. Already being treated like royalty, and that I was in love with the man.

It was pointed out by another cop that nothing had, in fact, been stolen, and there was no sign of foul play, or that I was trying to extort Victor. In the end, it was decided that I was in the wrong place at the wrong time, and the case, as far as I know, was still open.

Despite having just worked out with a client, I lit up a cigarette and sat in my car outside the police station. I inhaled deeply from the cigarette, knowing I was killing myself slowly, but loving every drag. I didn't smoke much. Only when I was nervous. And sitting outside the police station was harder on me than I thought it would be.

It had stopped raining. I was in a metered spot along the street just outside of the very police station made famous by a single Zsa Zsa Gabor slap. Traffic slogged past me. Rich people going home after making themselves richer. Water reflected off the road, off the cars. Red taillights and high-powered headlights reflected, too. Beverly Hills was a busy city. Lots of cars. Lots of people. Lots of business. Lots of money.

I finished the cigarette, flicked it out my side window like the bad girl I sometimes was, then got out and headed up to the station.

CHAPTER EIGHTEEN

After waiting nearly thirty minutes, I was shown into Detective Smithy's office.
Detective Smithy was a smallish man in a biggish office. His desk was polished. The window behind him appeared recently cleaned. I didn't detect any cobwebs or dirt or even dust bunnies. The computer monitor on his desk was bigger than my TV screen at home. Even the wires that led up to the monitor gleamed. I swear to God, someone had wiped those, too. Must be nice working for the Beverly Hills Police Department.

If Detective Smithy gave a damn about any of it, he didn't show it. His thick cop mustache was slightly askew. As in, I was fairly certain he didn't trim it as neat as his superiors would hope. His nails were mostly trimmed, except for his pinkie nail, which he seemed to have forgotten about. It was twice as long as the others. There was dirt under exactly half of the other nails. I suspected that what Detective Smithy lacked in grooming and hygiene, he more than made up for it in performance. At least, I hoped so.

When I came in, his smallish hand with the long pinkie nail was resting on top of a thick file. He didn't bother standing, but instead motioned to one of the three chairs sitting before him. I took the middle one because I enjoyed symmetry.

"What's your interest in this case, Ms. Lopez?" he asked while I straightened my workout pants so that the drape hung neatly. More symmetry. Then again, I think I was overcompensating for his lack of neatness with an overabundance of my own.

Detective Smithy looked at me as if I were doing something foreign to him, blinking once or twice. He waited. While he waited, I thought about how I should answer. Ultimately, I decided to go with the truth—the freaky truth—knowing there was a good chance I might be laughed out of the department.

"I was hired to help look for the killer," I said simply enough.

"I see," he said. "In what capacity?"

"I'm a psychic."

"A psychic?"

"A good one, too, although I'm new to murder investigations."

He didn't laugh. At least, not yet. Instead, he studied me closely. "I see. And where do you generally employ your services?"

Detective Smithy had an uncanny ability to look directly into me. Meaning, I knew he was sizing me up far differently than I was used to being sized up. The man was literally absorbing everything about me in ways that I suspected only a homicide cop could. What those ways were, I wasn't entirely sure, but judging from the way his eyes touched on every aspect of my face, my features, my clothing, there wasn't a whole lot this guy missed. Also, I intuitively sensed he was a hell of a fine detective.

"I work at the Psychic Hotline."

"The Psychic Hotline? Those guys I see on TV?"

"I'm one of those guys, or girls. There's a few of us, actually. I work out of my home, though. Callers get rerouted to me. They are, of course, in for a heck of a surprise when they get me."

Detective Smithy's smallish face with its slightly askew cop mustache didn't move much. But when I mentioned the Psychic Hotline, the errant whiskers twitched a little. "Oh?" he said. "What's the surprise?"

"I'm really good at what I do."

"I'm sure you are," he said, and this time his mustache didn't twitch. "May I ask who hired you?"

"Peter Laurie."

He stared at me. "Peter Laurie hired you?"

"Yes."

"The father of the victim?"

"Yes."

He continued staring at me long and hard and I sensed that something was amiss. Now he drummed his fingers and looked down at the file. He tilted his head a little and, there, his mustache actually looked straight.

"Is there something wrong?" I asked.

"There are many things wrong about the case, except I'm not at liberty to discuss them with you, Ms. Lopez."

"Peter said he was going to call you and give you permission to talk to me."

"Did he now?" said the detective.

"Yes. Didn't he call you?"

Detective Smithy held my gaze again, and I sensed a small energy shift in him. From one of rigidness and professionalism, to openness. He took in a lot of air, then finally nodded. "Yes, he did."

"And he said that you could speak to me."

"Yes, he did."

I sensed some of the detective's misgivings here. I said, "Except, of course, it's not his place to tell you who you can and can't talk to."

"True enough."

"But I want you to know that he did hire me—or tried to hire me. I told him I wouldn't take his money."

"How did you meet Mr. Laurie?"

"He called the Psychic Hotline."

"Did he request you specifically?"

I thought of Conn's efforts to reach me and nearly smiled. Instead, I shook my head and said, "You get who you get. It's all very random."

I thought of Millicent and wondered if she had something to do with my chance meeting with her son. I was betting that she had.

"I see," said the detective. "And you proceeded to meet with him later?"

"Yes, at his home. He showed me his daughter's room."

"Did he mention if any new evidence had come to light?"

"No. He just wanted a new…perspective on the case. I think I can give him that."

"Of course," said Detective Hill.

"You don't believe me," I said.

"I'm not sure what to believe, Ms. Lopez."

"Just give me a chance to help."

He looked at me sideways, fingers still drumming the case file, mind turning over rapidly, no doubt. Finally, he nodded. I sensed him tuning out, and about to shut me out, so I plunged in:

"I assure you, Detective. I'm good at what I can do, and I think I can help. I think I was meant to help, too."

He looked like a man who was certain he was about to make a very bad decision. Finally, reluctantly, painfully, he nodded. "Okay. Let's see what you can do, kiddo."

"Kiddo?"

"It's cop speak."

I smiled, and so did he. When he smiled, a few of the errant whiskers literally pointed directly at me. He said, "I've never worked with a psychic on a murder investigation."

"And I've never worked with a cop on one, either."

"I suppose I should give you access to this file, except that it's against the law for me to do so." He drummed his fingers on the file, thought about it. Then told me he would have his secretary sum up the file for me. I told him that was good enough.

"Come by tomorrow and it will be ready for you."

"Thank you, detective."

"What can I say? I'll do anything to catch this piece of shit. He destroyed a whole family. Perhaps many families."

On that note, he got up and led me over to the door. Once there, he said, "How is Peter doing these days? I haven't seen him since his wife died."

"Not good," I said. "Not good at all."

Detective Smithy was one inch taller than me. He held my gaze. Somehow, his cop mustache held my gaze, too. "No," he finally said, "I don't suspect he is."

CHAPTER NINETEEN

"Hi, this is Allison. Thank you for calling The Psychic Hotline. How can I help *you* see into the future?"

"Oh, thank the good lord in heaven," said Conn, and he sounded truly relieved.

"More than nine tries this time?" I asked. As I spoke, I immediately linked-up to him psychically. In a matter of moments, I saw him in my mind's eye sitting on his outdoor deck, this time in a robe and slippers. His robe was mostly closed. Conn had a majestic view of the Pacific Ocean. His home was surely worth millions.

I wondered if he knew that I could see him. Or, at least, suspected that I could see him. We'd never discussed my particular psychic strengths. In fact, we rarely, if ever, talked about anything psychic.

"Try *twenty* times," he said. He reached for a cup of coffee, sipped it. The coffee swirled with cream. Far below his house, along the beach, I heard people laughing and playing. What a life.

"Boy, you must really like talking to me," I said.

"You have no idea," he said.

"But why?" I asked. "Why do you keep calling me? We've never met. You have no idea what I look like."

"Before I answer that, can I ask if we are alone on the line?"

Good question. I did a quick scan and I felt that we were indeed alone. "We're good," I said. "So what gives?"

"You have a nice voice," he said.

"And that was enough?"

"That was a *start*," he corrected. "Do you remember why I called you initially?"

"It was about your mother," I said. "She'd recently passed."

"Yes, I had asked if you could tell me if she was okay. And you told me something I'd never expected to hear from an online psychic."

We were both silent. I remembered, of course, exactly what I had said. I waited for him, and as I did so, I felt a very, very loving energy wash over me.

"You said," he continued, "and I quote: 'I don't know.'"

He was right, of course. I didn't know. I'd never fancied myself a medium. I was primarily a remote viewer, with growing abilities in other areas. But, so far, no growth in medium-ship.

Unless, of course, one counted seeing a full-blown ghost in my living room medium-ship. Which I didn't. I could almost hear Millicent's words now: *Not a ghost, dear. Spirit. There is a difference.*

I said to Conn now, "Well, I wasn't going to lie to you or waste your money."

"But you could have," he said. "You could have told me anything, and I probably would have believed you."

I heard it in his voice...he was still looking for answers, or some type of validation that his mother was okay. Poor guy.

I said, "Well, that would have been wrong, and I'm not like that."

In my mind's eye, I saw Conn cross his arms over his chest, still holding his cell phone to his ear. He was wearing Ray-Ban sunglasses. Flecks of gray at his temples. He was tan and fairly toned. Okay, a lot toned. I already knew that, of course...but... it certainly looked like he'd been hitting the gym a little harder these days.

"And that was when it continued," said Conn.

"When *what* continued?" I asked.

"My, ah, interest in you."

"Lucky me," I said, although I smiled.

He smiled, too, and we spent a few minutes smiling at each other on the phone, except, of course, he didn't know I was smiling, and he didn't know I was watching him smile. As we sat there, with him absorbing the sun and working on his tan, and with me contemplating my morning cigarette, I had another loving sensation spill over me, this time followed by some words. I saw them, in fact, on a polished black tombstone: "Our Loving Rose."

Almost instantly, my heart picked up a beat or two. I sat forward, adjusting my headset, and nearly knocking my laptop off my lap. "Does the name Rose mean anything to you, Conn?"

The image of Conn had been replaced by the tombstone, but I sensed very strongly that Conn had sat up himself. "Rose is my mother's name. How did you know that?"

"Does...does her tombstone say 'Our Loving Rose'?"

There was a long pause. "How...How did you know that, Allison?"

"I just saw it."

I also saw him remove his sunglasses and bury his face in his hands. As he wept, I felt a wave of unconditional love, and I knew what it was and who it was for.

"Your mother, I think, is sending me love for you. A lot of love. More love than I've ever felt in all my life."

I had to stop because now the tears were coming and I couldn't speak, and Conn and I spent the next few minutes weeping silently over the phone.

CHAPTER TWENTY

It was late, and I'd been drinking.
I was sitting in the Spirit Chair with the police report summary, which I'd picked up earlier and had read a half-dozen times. There was something in there. Something that the police had either failed to see or had missed completely.

I let my subconscious work on that. Or my Higher Self, or whatever I wanted to call it. Some things couldn't be rushed. Some things were presented to us with perfect timing and it was our job to wait patiently, yet expectantly.

And I was very, very expectant that I would find an answer hidden within this summary.

Mostly, as I sat in the Spirit Chair, I was troubled. Troubled in a good way, perhaps. I was thinking about my experience with Conn. I'd never before shown signs of medium-ship and this was new to me.

Also, her love for him had been overwhelmingly pure and beautiful, and made me, on some level, wish I had a child of my own, to love so completely.

Of course, I needed a man for that, and I hadn't felt like dating since my last two disasters. And by *disasters*, I meant my last two relationships had ended horribly. Both men had been murdered.

One had been killed by a silver-tipped arrow. And my last boyfriend, a man I had been engaged to and still loved and was still having problems moving past, had been killed by what is known as a *dim-mak*, or in martial arts speak, a *death-blow*.

Crazy stuff, I know. But the pain was real. For both men. Well, one man and one vampire. Yes, my relationship with Victor had been pleasure-based, and we both sort of used each other, too, but I'd grown close to him quickly. Hell, instantly. And I missed him like crazy.

Caesar Marquez, my brave and sexy boxer, had been a different story. We had so much in common, and I had been certain he and I would grow old together, although I was always—*always*—nervous about boxing. Turned out, I had good reason to be. He and I had discussed kids, too. Building a family together, a life together.

Thinking of him now, especially after a few glasses of wine, wasn't a smart thing to do. The booze was liable to reduce me to tears for many hours, and leave me curled in the fetal position at the foot of my bed, or on the phone with Samantha, sobbing like a teenager while she made sympathetic noises. Samantha was a good friend, although it had taken her a while to come around. Same with me, I guessed. I didn't make friends easily, but when I did, well, I bonded with them forever.

So, I forced myself to think of something else...and ended up thinking of some*one* else.

Conn.

What was his deal? Who was he? I had resisted doing too much research on the man. Yes, I had made sure he wasn't a creep, but beyond that, I didn't know much about him, and I didn't *want* to know much about him. And if I was honest with myself, I would admit to the reason why: because I wanted him to tell me himself.

Perhaps over wine.

I sighed and shook my head and wiped the tears that had pooled in that small space between my upper cheekbone and lower eyelid.

Too soon, I thought. The pain of losing Caesar was still too raw. I needed more healing. A lot more healing. And with that thought, I was reminded about Conn's mother coming through.

Could I someday channel Caesar? I didn't know, but I suspected that seeing him, and feeling his love for me, knowing he was okay and still watching over me, my protector, might be enough for me to move on.

Might.

With a deep sigh, I pushed past the pain and opened the book in my lap. The book on Wicca, of course. Since, according to Millicent, I'd been a witch down through the ages.

I shook my head at the thought and wondered if I'd ever been burned at the stake. On second thought, I didn't want to know.

So, I went through the basic exercises again, practicing my visualization, practicing feeling the energy in various objects around me, including the array of crystals lined on my bookshelf behind me. I discovered I received an almost electric tingle—very similar to the feeling when Millicent appeared—when I held my hand over the chunk of amethyst.

I reveled in the feeling for a few minutes then went on to the other crystals. Each seemed to have a signature, a feeling, a buzzing, but none like the amethyst. According to the instruction book, I was to use whatever stone resonated the most with me for various spells and ceremonies. Well, then, amethyst it was!

And, no, I still had not wrapped my head around the thought of performing spells or participating in ceremonies. Truth was, other than mild interest, I'd never considered pursuing witchcraft, or Wicca, in the past. More truth, I never really believed in magic, either. Yes, I believed in extrasensory perception, but real magic? The ability to influence the physical through potions, ritual and intent?

No, I didn't think it was possible.

And yet...so much of Wicca I already performed without knowing it. Its practice of grounding oneself to Mother Earth prior to a reading. I did that. Grounding was necessary to maintain a deep connection to our greatest battery source: the Earth itself. I also practiced my own form of shielding, too. Yes, there were some negative energies and entities out there, and lately, I was feeling them more and more. Hell, I'd been possessed by such an entity.

A lot of what I was doing was similar to the Wiccan techniques. I'd been taught the grounding and shielding techniques in a class I'd taken years ago. Had the trainer been Wiccan? Were her psychic techniques influenced by Wicca, or was it the other way around? Or was there some cross-pollinating going on?

I didn't know, but reading through the Wiccan book felt... comfortable. It also felt like I had sort of come home.

I continued through the exercises, feeling like I was mastering each quickly as I went. Maybe I was a natural at this stuff. Maybe I really had been a witch in a past life.

And a very good one, Daughter.

I glanced up, gasping. "Millicent?" I asked.

I doubted she was here, though, because I didn't feel that same electrical charge when she made her presence known.

Oh, she is near, overseeing your instruction, as are a few others.

My heart thumped. The words appeared directly in my thoughts. I was sure of it. I was also sure they weren't from Millicent, either.

"Who are you?"

For an answer, I saw a primeval forest, with huge, majestic pines rising high into the sky, and ferns crowding everywhere. I saw birds flitting from branch to branch, squirrels running up and down trunks. I saw moss and mushrooms and rotted logs and trails and deer. The image morphed into churning seas with misty land rising in the far distance. I saw ships on the horizon, and then my view dipped down below the waves and there I saw all manner of aquatic life. The ocean floor segued into wind-blown desert dunes. I saw caravans and tents and camels. I saw oases and awe-inspiring sandstorms. From there, I was led high up into snow-covered peaks. Below me was the world, shrouded in fog, and teeming with life. Above all else, I sensed unending, boundless, pure love for it all. A mother's love.

"You are..." but my voice faltered.

Call me Gaia, said the quiet but strong voice in my head, and I felt her love for me, too.

Mother Earth.

CHAPTER TWENTY-ONE

I felt very strongly that I should sit back, relax, and close my eyes.
So, I did that now. Within seconds, I was in a deeply meditative state. I felt like I was floating. Most important, I felt detached from my own body. I'd done this before, entered a trance-like state. But never so quickly and deeply.

You are Mother Earth, I thought.
I've been called many things, but I do have a name.
Gaia, I thought.
Yes. We all have spiritual names, child.
And what's mine?
It will be revealed to you at another time.

I nodded, although I knew my physical body never moved. I nodded within my own mind, or wherever it was that I had gone.

You are with me, said Gaia.
I don't understand.
Look around you.

I did. I was surrounded by molten walls, iridescent and glowing and beautiful. The molten metals churned and roiled. That my body was sitting comfortably in the Spirit Chair in my bedroom in Beverly Hills seemed almost a distant memory.

I am much more than the surface you see, my daughter. As are you.
My Higher Self, I said.
Yes. Your current physical form is just a small representation of who you really are.

And who am I, really?

A part of God.

Are you God? I asked.

I'm a part of God as well. Perhaps a slightly bigger part. I heard light chuckling in my head.

A lot of people worship you. They call you the Earth Mother, or Earth goddess.

Worship and respect are sometimes interchangeable and often confused.

Should you be worshipped?

Worship only God's glory through me.

The scene shifted from under the earth, and soon I found myself upon a stony crag high above a many-layered canyon. Below, a narrow strip of water wended its way through the steep cliffs, cutting through the stone as it had done for eons upon eons. I was hundreds of feet up, and the narrow strip, I soon realized, was actually a raging river. The sun was warm on my face. The wind was cool on my neck.

You are all of this? I asked.

We are all part of the Creator, child. But, yes, the earth is my physical shell, if you will.

You inhabit the Earth, as I inhabit my own physical body?

This is true.

So, you are not very different from me?

We are all from the Creator, but there are some of us who are created for different purposes.

I thought about that. *Such as other planets?*

And stars and moons and galaxies and universes and other heavenly bodies.

My head was spinning. *You were created, then, for the specific purpose of inhabiting the Earth?*

Partially true. I have been other planets throughout time and space. The Earth, I'll admit, has been one of my favorites.

What is your role for us? I asked. *For humanity?*

I was still standing on the rocky ledge, but now I sensed a presence nearby. Mostly, I sensed a gathering of energy next to me. It was *her*, of course, Mother Earth. Focusing her energy, although she was without shape or form. No, not true...before me, everywhere, was her shape and form, from the rocks to the trees, to the rivers to the beaches.

My role is to help you evolve, child. To help all of you evolve upon my surface and under it.

Under it?

I sensed her smile next to me. *That is a conversation for another time.*

But how do you help us evolve?

By giving you a playground to live in, to work in, to love in, to experience physical life in. I work closely with, shall we say, higher energies.

Higher energies? I'd come across the concept in some of my readings, that many masters walk the Earth, both in physical and non-physical forms, helping those who seek them and God.

I sensed her nod next to me. *Highly evolved beings, yes. There is, you see, an experiment going on, although few of you know it.*

An experiment? I didn't like the sound of that.

The Earth, and other planets like me, are conducting a free-will experiment, if you will.

I don't understand.

You have all been given free will, to do as you wish, to conduct yourselves as you wish, to do with me as you wish, to others as you wish. The Creator wants to see what you will make of yourselves, and with me. The Creator wants to see if you will fly or fall.

Doesn't the Creator know all? I asked. Doesn't the Creator know what will happen?

There are many possible outcomes, and many of them are known to me, as well, as are they known to the spiritual masters.

The highly evolved beings.

Yes. Which is why they are here to help.

But if they are helping, I asked, *then doesn't that remove our free will?*

A good, question, child. Consider it loving nudges, but only for those who call upon them and seek them out with love.

This is hurting my head, I said.
Then I suggest we end this meditation with a dive off my cliff.
I looked down into the sparkling silvery thread far below.
Won't I die?
You are sitting in your Spirit Chair, are you not?
True, I said, and laughed.
Then jump, daughter. I am waiting for you with open arms.

I hesitated for only a moment, then closed my eyes and leaped off the ledge. I arched up and out, suspended briefly in mid-air, then dropped like a rock. The water approached rapidly, and as it did, I straightened my body and aimed head first, hands together before me, and plunged into the ice-cold water. Bubbles swarmed around me as I sank deeper and deeper.

I gasped and opened my eyes, and found myself back in my bedroom, in the Spirit Chair, breathing hard and gripping the amethyst charm.

How it got into my hand, I didn't know.

CHAPTER TWENTY-TWO

I was nervous. Damn nervous.

It was the next morning, and I was still thinking about my experience with Mother Earth, digesting her concepts, and, most of all, feeling her love, when I pulled up to the last place that Penny Laurie had been seen alive: her elementary school.

I was here because of a dream. I'd dreamed I was in a clover field, sitting with Penny. She was nearby, painting a cute picture of Ren, from *The Ren & Stimpy Show*, which was a kind of a dog, I supposed. A chihuahua, I think. We were sitting quietly as she painted. All around us, bees were buzzing and birds were tweeting, and that's when I woke up.

But I didn't get up immediately. No, I'd spent many minutes in bed, thinking long and hard about the meaning of the dream, then finally decided to see what the dream could mean. I went straight to my dream dictionary and did my best to interpret the many images, but nothing seemed to resonate. Not the bees nor the dog nor the clover field. Nothing.

No, not quite nothing.

I dashed through my apartment and found the police summary of Penny's case. In particular, the school she had gone to.

The last place she had been seen alive.

Her school was called, of course, Clover Field Elementary.

I parked in the visitor parking and wondered what the hell I was going to do next.

It made sense to retrace her footsteps to the last place she'd been seen alive. Except the police had done that. Anyone who was anyone, from fellow classmates to teachers, from the principal to the crosswalk guard, had been thoroughly interviewed. In fact, I'd read a summary of all of the interviews, and they all read the same: Penny had left school at the same time she always had to make the two-block walk to her home, which was literally just down the street. She had been in fifth grade, and her parents had deemed her old enough to safely walk home the short distance.

Of course, she had never made it home.

I stepped out of my car. The morning had warmed up considerably. The school itself had a high fence around it that looked like serious business. It also looked new. Penny's murder might have had something to do with that.

I moved through the parking lot, reaching out psychically, trying to get a feel, a hit, anything. Nothing yet, but I was in the right place, I was sure of it. Lots of Mercedes and BMWs in the parking lot. Since when did teachers get paid so well?

I followed a footpath that led along the wrought iron fence, and walked toward the nearby residential street. Beyond the fence were rows of school buildings and an open grass field, complete with backstops and baseball diamonds. The school itself was quiet and peaceful. An airplane droned high overhead. That a girl had been abducted from here and murdered and discarded in a nearby playground was nearly incomprehensible.

Someone knows something.

At the quiet street, I looked to my left where the road curved slightly. Just two blocks from here was Penny's home, now presently out of view. In view, however, were dozens of beautiful mini-mansions. Some might have even been full-blown mansions.

The last witness to see her had been the crossing guard, an elderly woman who had led her, along with two or three other kids, across the street.

Penny had disappeared around the curve and out of view... and into oblivion.

As I stood here on the street, with the school behind me, I spied the current crosswalk guard sitting in a foldout chair with a small umbrella attached to it. This crosswalk guard was now a middle-aged man.

I sighed and chewed my lower lip. Penny had been in fifth grade. Those students would have all moved on to the nearby middle school. That left, of course, only one person who could tell me more about Penny's last day.

Her teacher.

I remembered his name from the report. Mr. Fletcher, or William Fletcher.

"Mr. Fletcher," I said aloud.

Saying the name now sent a small shiver up and down my spine. Seeing the name in the report hadn't done much for me, although I always had a sense that I would eventually talk to him about the case. The police had been highly interested in him, as well, but he'd fully checked out. He'd been seen at school during the time Penny had walked home, during the time she would have been abducted.

I closed my eyes, and felt the wind on my face and saw her now in the clover field, picking flowers, not looking at me, her face sullen.

She looked mad. This was probably how she looked when she last saw her mother. They'd had a fight, of course, and that was the reason for the mother's guilt, the reason the mother, eventually, had killed herself.

Perhaps Penny had felt too bad about the quarrel to go straight home? Perhaps she had still been angry with her mother, and wanted to brood about it elsewhere?

I thought about that as I headed back to my car. I checked the time. Almost eleven. School would be out in four hours. I would come back.

To talk to Mr. Fletcher.

CHAPTER TWENTY-THREE

I was at a Starbucks with a ghost.
Okay, not a ghost, as she liked to point out, but a spirit. Millicent was standing nearby, her hands properly folded in front of her, looking about as old—or young—as me. That is mid-thirties.

You're looking good these days, I thought.
It is the age and appearance I most closely associate with myself.

Truth was, she looked nothing like the old photographs in Peter's house...but also different. In fact, she looked even more tantalizingly familiar.

It is the form I had when last I was your sister.
And when was that?
Two lifetimes ago.

You're weird, I thought, and gave her, I supposed, a very sisterly grin.

Of course, anyone looking at me would have thought I was just grinning at the book, that I had found something in the Wicca primer as funny. That was actually very much not the case. I found the book enchanting, no pun intended. The spells, the potions, the lifestyle, the festivals, the sabbats or holidays, all felt familiar, comfortable, something I knew in my heart I had done before, and had experienced often.

Although familiar, I had no direct access to my past lives, at least not at this time in my life. Probably a good thing, too. Life was challenging enough as it was.

Can other people see you? I telepathically asked Millicent.

One or two can feel me, but that's about it.

Indeed, a woman sitting not too far away glanced over at me often, and rubbed her arms. She was, I suspected, a sensitive-in-training, whether she knew it or not.

That I was about to meet Penny's teacher later today made me nervous. I wasn't a trained investigator. I didn't know what I would say to him, or even how to go about saying it. All I knew was that the more I thought about him, the more I didn't like him.

I'm meeting Penny's teacher today.

I'm well aware that you are about to meet the teacher. We all are.

We? I asked.

Your helpers, dear.

My guides?

Yes, of course.

Does he know something?

There is a natural order to all that is, dear. A natural order to revelation, as well.

And to justice? I asked.

Yes, dear. The timing had not been right.

Until now? I asked, but she remained silent about that. She did that to me, and it was aggravating. And since she was in spirit and not detailed enough for me to read her expressions, I had to accept her silence, although I didn't like it.

I sighed and returned to the book, in particular, to a section that had piqued my interest earlier. It discussed telekinesis, and something about the subject sent a jolt through me.

According to the Wicca primer, few had the ability of telekinesis—that was, to move objects with one's mind—but, with years of work and arduous study and applying oneself diligently, one could possibly develop a trace of this ability.

As I read the section again and again, I sensed a growing excitement in me. Now, why was that?

Because, child, you have put in the work already.

I looked at Millicent, who was now standing before me, next to a woman in line. The woman kept looking behind herself, rubbing her neck and shivering.

What do you mean? I asked.

You have spent lifetimes perfecting telekinesis.

Little good that does me now.

Not true, dear. Your higher self remembers all the lessons. It's imprinted in you, permanently, waiting for you to explore it again. To summon it again. You would be what many call a prodigy.

Is that why prodigies are so gifted at a young age? I asked, sitting back. This was a new concept for me.

Exactly, dear. They were masters in previous incarnations. It doesn't take much to awaken their soul memory. And it won't take much for you, either.

I thought about that...and the excitement continued to grow. Was it possible? I didn't know, but the book pointed out that telekinesis went beyond just moving objects with one's mind. Advanced telekinesis, as performed by true masters, also involved *creating* objects from the ether-sphere. No, not quite the ether-sphere. From the God energy that permeated everything. The energy was there, waiting to be used, waiting to be manipulated, waiting to be formed into something new, something powerful, something beautiful.

This was heavy stuff, and just the thought that I might have mastered some of this stuff was exciting in and of itself.

Anyway, the book suggested a simple exercise to test one's current level of telekinesis. But don't get your hopes up, the book cautioned, as few would see results, and those who did were in a rarefied group.

Rarefied...I liked that.

I almost smiled.

Okay, I did smile.

Broadly.

Anyway, the book suggested taking out your keys and placing them before you. Keys held a lot of spirit energy, residual energy, as they were often in contact with people, and held a special connection to home and health and valuables and protection.

I did so now, taking out my rather thick ring of keys from my oversized handbag. Yes, I'm a girl. I placed the wad of keys on the table before me. The whole shebang clattered loudly, as well they should. It was a big wad.

Next, I cleared my thoughts, focused my intent, exerted my loving will onto the physical world, and saw in my mind's eye the atoms and energy rearrange themselves in accordance with my desire.

At least, that was the plan.

I did this again and again, and waited for something to happen. Nothing did. Oh, well.

Patience, child, came Millicent's words. *Now try again. Go deeper.*

But I am at a Starbucks.

God is in Starbucks, too, don't you know?

Well, we all need our coffee, I thought.

I closed my eyes and tried again, and did my best to tune out the chattering and the tapping of keyboards, of the door opening and closing, of people laughing and kids playing. Yes, it was a busy Starbucks. A minute or two later—or perhaps longer, hard to know with meditation—a peaceful bliss came over me. I was deep. At least, as deep as I could hope for in the land of coffee.

Now, I saw the keys in my mind's eye, glowing softly, surrounded by what very easily could have been God energy. Then again, what did I know? With eyes still closed and my physical hands still in my lap, I mentally reached out and took hold of the keys. Why I did this, I didn't know. Something within me just knew that to do this exercise correctly, I needed to reach out mentally.

I did so now, seeing my ethereal hand grab hold of the keys, and as I did so in my mind, I heard the keys in the real world move ever so slightly. A small scraping sound on the table.

Good, child. Good.

Heart thumping and excitement swelling within me, I held the image of me mentally holding the keys as I opened my eyes. It was this dichotomy of telekinesis, I knew, that tripped up so many would-be practitioners: that of holding a mental image of the object...and also seeing it in real time.

But I seemed to hold the image easily enough.

And now, in my mind, I turned the keys...and on the table, as if manipulated by an invisible hand, the keys turned in real-time, too. In fact, they performed a perfect 360-degree turn.

I broke the connection and sat back. "Holy shit," I whispered.

Watch your language, dear, said Millicent in my head, *but you can say that again.*

I smiled...and then I was laughing.

Almost hysterically.

CHAPTER TWENTY-FOUR

School was out.

They piled out in droves, laughing and running with their oversized backpacks. An ungodly long line of minivans and SUVs wended its way through school. Yes, some kids even walked home, although I sure as hell wouldn't have let my own kid walk home. Not from this school, and not with a killer still on the loose.

I watched it all from the parking lot, from within my humble Honda Accord, looking, no doubt, like just another anxious mother. Of course, I was anxious for an entirely different reason. Perhaps even an unwarranted reason. I was going to speak to Penny's fifth-grade teacher, Mr. Fletcher, and I was nervous as hell.

No, I hadn't received a strong psychic hit that he was actually involved. But I knew I needed to speak to him, and I would.

I just didn't like it.

I was, after all, just a telephone psychic and part-time personal trainer. I didn't confront people, especially about murder. Yes, I could have called my private eye friend, Samantha Moon. She would have come out here for me. But it was afternoon, and she would have been picking up her own kids slathered in sunscreen and dressed in a lot of clothes to protect her from the sun. Besides, I wanted to talk to the bastard here, now, in the classroom. I wanted to size him up for myself, get a feel of him for myself, and then take it from there. Wherever *there* would lead.

Feeling strongly that there was a good chance Penny hadn't headed home, that she had gone somewhere to sulk about Mommy being mean that day opened up the possibility that anyone could have come across her. Even Mr. Fletcher, whose alibi was airtight.

So, where were my friendly spirits now? Why did I suddenly feel so alone?

I knew the answer, of course.

They were nearby. They were watching me with extreme interest. The Universe wanted justice, needed justice. A karmic balance needed to be met. A girl had been murdered and a family had been torn apart. Karmic suffering had been great and the world, quite literally, was out of balance because of it.

Whether or not I could provide that balance, I didn't know. Had no clue, in fact. But one thing was certain: I was going to have to go about this mostly on my own, using as many psychic hits as I could to help me along the way.

I drummed my polished nails on the hot steering wheel. My nails looked sexy. At least, that's what I'd always thought. My nails were also expensive, and rooted in materialism and appearance.

Well, dammit, I certainly wasn't as flashy as the other girls out here. And, well, I *liked* nice nails. Nails made me feel good about myself, and, I figured, feeling good about oneself should be *paramount*. Plus, I had a famous zip code to live up to.

So be it.

My car was heating up so I rolled down the windows. Buses came and went, and so did moms in SUVs. Some dads, too, in bigger trucks. Of course, the SUVs here were Porsches and Range Rovers and Escalades. Everything was big and polished, much like many of the moms. Everyone wore sunglasses. I did, too, of course. Hey, it was bright in Beverly Hills!

When the parade of polished cars and people were over, when most of the students had been picked up and as a smattering of teachers talked together, laughing, clearly relieved that another day had come and gone, I stepped out of my Accord, locked it with a *beep*, adjusted my sunglasses, and took a deep breath, And then, I went looking for Mr. Fletcher.

Thanks to the police summary, I knew just where to find him.

CHAPTER TWENTY-FIVE

"Hi, are you Mr. Fletcher?"

A man in his early thirties turned from the dry-erase board where he'd just written tomorrow's date. Very efficient. He was also very handsome. He was not much bigger than my own 5'7", although he had broad shoulders and clearly worked out. He was dressed in a light blue polo shirt and snug jeans. He wore designer Timberland boots that probably stopped somewhere at the ankle. He looked at once dashing and relaxed.

"You got him," he said, recapping his dry-erase pen and setting it in the grooved metal slot at the base of the board. He next picked up an eraser. Had I not been standing in the doorway, he would have gone to town erasing various mathematical problems that looked, sad to say, too difficult even for me to puzzle out at first blush. Since when did kids get so damned smart? Instead, he waited for me with a pleasant smile on his handsome face. "How can I help you?"

"Do you have a few minutes to talk?"

"I do, if you don't mind if I clean up a little while we speak."

"I don't mind."

"Then fire away," he said, and began quickly working his way down the dry-erase board, wiping it clean as if magically.

I didn't know where to begin, so I said lamely, "Whatever happened to good old chalkboards?"

"They went the way of the dodo," he said, looking at me over his shoulder as he wiped. He tried to grin, but it came out awkwardly. I sensed he didn't smile much, and as I stood here in the classroom, I got a very strong sense that he was a severe teacher, a strict disciplinarian. I reached out psychically to the classroom itself and sensed real fear here. Yes, his students were afraid of him. The teacher that no one wanted to have, despite his good looks.

I said, "Well, we had chalkboards when I was a kid, and I turned out fine. Just ask my therapist."

Now he did chuckle lightly, but, again, it seemed forced. "Same here, but that's progress for you. I've never seen you before. Are you a parent?"

"No," I said, and now the nerves kicked in again, especially when I realized the significance of who he might be. "But I hope to be. You know, someday."

He looked at me oddly as he returned the eraser to the metal tray at the base of the board. I would have looked at me oddly, too.

"So, what can I do for you?" He had moved over to his desk where he'd begun gathering paperwork and tucking it neatly into a file carrying case.

I took in a lot of air. And I mean *a lot*. I held it and suddenly wished I was anywhere else but here. My God, I was a psychic at the Psychic Hotline. A personal trainer. I was good at both jobs. I didn't confront people. I didn't, in fact, know what the hell I was doing.

So, I did the only thing I could think of. I plunged right in, perhaps stupidly or perhaps even bravely. I said, "I'm here about Penny Laurie."

He didn't miss a beat. He continued shoving papers into his file holder. Or was he shoving them in a little harder now? With a little more vigor, perhaps? Probably not, but after a few seconds of what I thought was him clearly thinking through the situation, he began shaking his head sadly.

"A tragedy," he said, still shaking his head. Still shoving papers in his file.

To me, his reaction wasn't normal. Although not a trained investigator but a human who had seen her fair share of people on this planet, I felt that his reaction was *calculated.*

Or maybe I had convinced myself that this guy was bad news, and was looking for anything to validate that assumption.

Maybe.

Or perhaps, I was just frustrated that I wasn't getting any help from Millicent. Hell, even from Penny herself. No, I wasn't a medium, but that certainly hadn't stopped Millicent from reaching out to me.

I needed help here. I was in over my head.

But I wasn't getting it. It was just me and Mr. Fletcher, and my own psychic intuition. My specialty of remote viewing wouldn't do me much good here. But my other, less reliable, skills were letting me know that there was something here to be wary of.

I could feel the latent buried within the classroom walls, the desks, the carpeted floor. Fear, I knew, had an energy signature that imprints deeply into the environment. So did love. So did death.

But it was fear that I was feeling now.

"Yes, a tragedy," I said, heart racing.

"I'm sorry," said Mr. Fletcher, finally looking up from his folder. He idly held a stack of papers in his hand. "Who are you again?"

"I'm a friend of the family," I said. Yes, I had thought long and hard about just how to answer that very question. It was the best reply I had.

"Like I said," he said, shaking his head sadly, "it's a tragedy, but I do need to get going soon."

"You were one of the last adults to see her alive, Mr. Fletcher, so do you mind if I ask you a few questions?"

"Actually, I do. Her murder has troubled me deeply, and, quite frankly, I haven't been the same since. I would rather not open old wounds."

Now, he shoved the entire bulging file folder into a leather satchel, which he slung over one shoulder. He was leaving and he wasn't talking. I knew I needed to say something that would keep him talking or get some kind of a reaction from him. "I'm sorry to open old wounds, Mr. Fletcher."

Now he was coming toward me. His shoulders seemed broader now, and he certainly didn't look like any teacher I would want my kids to have, if I had kids.

But I stood my ground, standing before the door and blocking it. "As it turned out, she didn't go directly home after school."

He said nothing, just continued coming toward me.

"I suspect she went to a nearby park, perhaps even the park she was dumped in. You see, she was mad at her mom, and didn't want to go home. Maybe she thought she would be punished if she went home. I believe she was at this park when she met her killer, a man."

He stopped before me. He was shaking and doing all he could to control himself. His nostrils flared out. That he had anger issues was an understatement. "And you know this how?"

"I'm a psychic, Mr. Fletcher."

He didn't laugh. He didn't shrug it off. He didn't do anything that one might expect.

Instead, his eyes darkened and he seemed to lower his shoulders a little more. He wanted to attack, I sensed it, could feel it, see it. And if he did, I knew there was nothing I could do to protect myself. Or, mostly nothing. I still had a knee, and he still had a groin.

Instead, after a moment of staring me down with nothing but hate, he said, "Watch your back."

Then he brushed past me, and was gone.

CHAPTER TWENTY-SIX

I was shaking.
Shaking and shaken. *Jesus,* I thought, as I headed back to my car. *Had I just confronted a killer? A real killer?*

I had; I was certain of it.

My legs were still feeling a bit wobbly as I passed teachers and other staff walking the various hallways, and passed the occasional errant kid who was, I suspected, here for some after-school program or other. The parking lot was mostly empty, too, although there was a smattering of cars and some kids hanging out near the front entrance with a stern-looking woman. Late parents, I suspected. The woman, who had a very vice-principally feel to her, wasn't pleased.

Where Mr. Fletcher had gone off to, I didn't know, but as I drew closer to the parking lot, and as the stern-looking woman turned to glance at me, a cold wind blasted over me. And I mean *blasted.* I shivered violently. The stern woman frowned at me. Apparently, shivering was frowned upon at Clover Field Elementary.

I'd experienced such sensations before, and many of my psychic friends would tell me that such unexpected blasts of cold air were spirit activity. I didn't know, but I appeared to be the only one affected. I smiled weakly at the woman and slipped past her and the kids and into the parking lot.

Samantha Moon had told me that she possessed a sort of inner warning system. A warning system that actually sounded in her head when danger was near. I suspected that all vampires had this, as, according to her, it was the earliest indicator that she had any psychic abilities. I didn't have such an audible warning system. But something was going on with me now. Most notably, the hair on my arms was standing on end.

'Watch your back,' Mr. Fletcher had said.

As I moved through the parking lot, aware that something was happening around me, aware that the very air around me seemed to be crackling with electrical energy—spirit energy—I shoved my hands in my pockets, hunched my shoulders and headed for my Accord.

Something's going to happen, I suddenly thought.

I was on high alert, reaching out with all the psychic skills I had. Most curious was that I was feeling a buildup in energy around me. A different kind of energy. Nature energy. Universal energy. It was gathering around me, swarming around, filling me.

What the hell is happening?

Somewhere nearby, I heard a car's engine rev loudly. Wait, not nearby.

Directly behind me.

I spun in time to see a Ford Mustang peel around a turn in the parking lot. Although the windows were tinted, I could still see Mr. Fletcher behind the wheel.

The car came at me shockingly fast, bounding, veritably leaping forward. I could dive to the side, yes, but he could turn the steering wheel, too.

I had seconds to decide, and, really, it wasn't much of a decision.

I did what came to me naturally.

What had come to me naturally throughout time and space, throughout lifetimes and incarnations. I gathered the surrounding energy that had been building around me, waiting to be used, ready to be used.

I gathered it and stood my ground, and as the car approached, and as the driver's eyes widened with both alarm and pleasure, I threw my hands forward and released the energy.

I wasn't prepared for what was to come.

Yes, I was a witch. Yes, I had developed those skills in past lives, over the centuries. But that didn't mean I knew what was going to happen in *this* life.

And boy, did it happen.

Raw power blasted from me like a cannon shot. I couldn't see it, but I could feel it. I saw it as a shield in my mind, and that's exactly what it was.

An invisible shield.

The Mustang slammed into it, or rather, it slammed into the Mustang—I was never sure which—but either way, the front end of the vehicle crumpled completely. The back end lifted up… and Mr. Fletcher, who wasn't wearing his seat belt, went flying through the front windshield.

CHAPTER TWENTY-SEVEN

I was in the back of Detective Smithy's squad car.

William Fletcher's body still lay on the concrete, in exactly the position I'd left him in after I'd rolled him over, after I tried, unsuccessfully, to stop the blood that pumped from the gash in his neck. He had gone through the window face-first. The windshield had won. The blood pooled instantly, and he was dead within minutes, bleeding out, despite my best efforts.

I wept throughout, as did the other teachers nearby, some of whom were shrieking and doing all they could to keep the remaining students away.

The squad car door opened and Detective Smithy slid in next to me. He pulled the door shut gently and looked at me. I was staring down at my hands, at the blood under my now-broken index fingernail. I absently picked under it, flicking the congealed hemoglobin away as Smithy silently watched me.

"You okay?" He'd already asked me that a dozen times, and so had the paramedics. No one, apparently, could believe I wasn't hurt.

"I'm fine."

Again, he didn't believe me. No one believed me. "What happened out there?"

"He tried to run me down."

"Fletcher?"

"He's the one who's dead, isn't he?"

Smithy nodded. Homicide detectives, I figured, rarely got their feelings hurt. "Why?"

"Because I implicated him in the murder of Penny Laurie."

Smithy continued staring at me. I continued picking at my nails. Outside, a child cried incessantly. More cop cars appeared. A fire truck. Dozens, if not hundreds, of bystanders. Smithy and I were mostly hidden within a circle of Beverly Hills finest.

"What evidence do you have?" he asked.

I'd been having a hard time thinking straight. I'd gone into a sort of shock, while sitting there on the ground shaking and fighting for breath while a man bled out near my feet.

Not just a man. A *child killer*.

"Nothing that would stand up in court."

"So, tell me about it."

I did, as best as I could. I told him about the dream and the clover field. That Penny might not have been on her way home at all, that she might have, in fact, gone to a nearby park to sulk and think and to silently hate her mother in the way that only a ten-year-old girl could.

"You don't think she was picked up on the way home from school?" he said.

"No, I don't."

"But she always went straight home, every day. This has been corroborated."

"Not that day."

"How can you be so sure?"

For the first time, I looked at him. "I'm not sure."

"And you decided to come here alone?"

"Yes."

"That was reckless." He refrained from saying *stupid*. Why kick a girl when she was down?

I nodded, feeling sick all over again. "I had to know for sure."

"And do you know for sure?"

I held his gaze. His eyes were bigger than I remembered. "Without a doubt."

"Without a single doubt, you believe that William Fletcher killed Penny Laurie?"

"Yes."

"Did he say as much?"

"He threatened me," I said. "Then followed up on his threat."

Smithy took in a lot of air, and his little man-child chest filled up. No, he wasn't a big man, but he had a big presence. "We'll check him out thoroughly."

I nodded. "Good."

I pressed my thumb and fingers into my closed eyes, doing my best to soothe a thumping headache, and saw an image of a blue box buried in Mr. Fletcher's back yard, under a flat marking stone. I also saw inside the box and my heart sank.

Find the dog, and you will find your answers.

With a heavy heart, I told the detective about the box, finishing with, "I think you'll find all the evidence you need inside."

"Inside the box?"

"Yes."

"Under a stone?"

"Yes."

"In Fletcher's back yard?"

I nodded, exhausted. "Yes, detective."

"Should I ask how you know this?"

"It just came to me."

"Of course it did. And why wouldn't the killer's identity just come to you, too?"

"Because that's not how this stuff works."

"It's not?"

"No, apparently not," I said.

"Explain it to me, then."

"Can I explain it another time?" I asked, rubbing my temples now. "I need a shower and to sleep and a place to cry for the rest of the night."

"First, give me the Cliffs Notes version," he said, "then you can cry all you want."

I sighed, rubbed my eyes again, and said, "Some things have to play out, Detective. They have to play out naturally, in their correct place and time. The spirit world does not exist to give us answers all the time, whenever we need them. We are forced to live a little, to experience a little, and to discover on our own, with occasional prodding from the other side; that is, if we go too far down the wrong path."

Smithy blinked exactly three times over a course of about a minute, before he said, "That might have been the craziest thing I've ever heard, but…"

He paused. I waited.

"…but it just might make some sense."

"It does," I said, "in a way."

"So, what happened with Fletcher? I mean, how did he go from running you down to outside his window and dead? And how did you not get hit? Every witness claims they saw you get hit."

"I wasn't hit," I said.

"Then what happened?"

"I can't tell you," I said.

"I really think you should."

I looked at him and shook my head. "I can't, Detective. Not now."

"Why?"

"Because I'm not sure what happened myself."

"I'm going to need more than that for my report, Ms. Lopez."

I shook my head again. "You'll get the answer someday. Maybe."

He didn't like it, but he kept it to himself, which I appreciated. We were both silent. Outside, we heard excitable voices, officers barking orders, and saw a whole lot of curious faces. Something else occurred to me.

"Will you be talking to Peter Laurie about this?" I asked.

Smithy looked at me for a long moment, his mustache twitching ever so slightly. His piercing eyes softened, and he said, "About Peter Laurie…"

CHAPTER TWENTY-EIGHT

I rapped on the front door.
I had come unannounced, which, under the circumstances, I had thought was best. I waited, and as I did so, I scanned the yard, noting again its perfectly manicured lawn and well-maintained garden. I noted again the "For Sale" sign out front, and the Realtor's lock box attached to a nearby water pipe. It was attached, in fact, to the water handle, which was currently pointing down in the "off" position. Which meant, of course, the interior of the house had no water, either.

I was about to knock again, when I heard heavy footsteps approach from the other side. With each slow step, my heart increased in tempo. As it did so, that familiar, electrical current formed around me, that tell-tale sign that a spirit was nearby.

Who's here with me? I asked.

I didn't, of course, get an answer, although I suspected I knew exactly who was here.

The door opened slowly and there stood Peter Laurie, as tall and forlorn and miserable as ever. As far as I knew, Peter had no knowledge of the events that had happened just hours earlier at Clover Field Elementary.

It had taken me a few hours to get here. I had to shower and cry and get dressed and cry some more. I had never, ever seen someone die before. Even a sicko child killer. It had been too much. Just too damn much.

Hell, it was still too much.

Anyway, I had needed to be alone, and then I'd needed to make a few phone calls.

"A lovely surprise, Ms. Lopez," said Peter with his usual warmth. Ever the gentleman.

"I hope I didn't disturb you," I said, stepping inside as he ushered me in.

He was, of course, wearing the same suit and tie. I had thought the man had dressed impeccably, or didn't have much variation to his wardrobe. I had thought wrong.

We were standing in the foyer. The spiral staircase was before us. The paintings were everywhere, as were the statues. Nothing had been touched. Peter was still holding his stomach. I motioned to it. "Are you feeling any better?"

"I wish I could say yes, but, sadly, no. I really should go see a doctor."

"How long has the pain been going on now?"

He looked at me, blinked, shrugged. "Why, I don't know. Quite a long time, I suppose. I really should go see a doctor."

"Yes, you just said that."

"Did I?"

"Yes."

He blinked at me, and sighed. "Let me tell you, my memory isn't holding up well these days."

"I'm sorry to hear that," I said. "So, why don't you go to the doctor, Peter?"

"I just..." he shrugged again, gave me a long look. "I just don't care enough, I suppose."

"You don't care enough about your own health?"

"Nothing much matters to me anymore. Not since..."

His voice trailed off and I nodded. He didn't need to finish his sentence. I knew what followed "not since..."

I said, "Tell me, Mr. Laurie, why are you moving?"

He looked at me for another long moment. "The house...it's so big...and I'm all alone now...surrounded by painful memories. I need to start somewhere fresh. I need to move on, I guess."

I nodded. I couldn't have agreed more. "Do you still go to work, Mr. Laurie?"

"I thought I'd told you I'd taken a leave of absence. Didn't I tell you that? Boy, I really can't remember much these days." He rubbed his face, moving his hand over the same three-day growth he'd been sporting for the past two weeks. His hand moving over his whiskers, I noticed, didn't make any sound. "Are you here with news about my daughter?" he asked.

"I found your daughter's killer today."

He snapped his eyes up, inhaled sharply. He seemed about to take my hand, or grab me about the shoulders, or perform some other form of physical contact, but refrained. He was, of course, the perfect gentleman. Or something. "Please, Allison, tell me who it is. Tell me everything."

And so I did. I told him all about my dream, about the connection to her school, about my theory that Penny never went straight home. I told him about my meeting with her teacher. I paused there and Peter Laurie seemed to be holding his breath. Tears came to his eyes and then spilled down his cheeks.

"Her teacher?" he asked finally.

I nodded and relayed the conversation I'd had with Mr. Fletcher...and then the attack in parking lot. As I spoke, I felt nauseated, knowing that a man was dead by my hand...a man who'd died only hours ago.

Sweet Jesus, help me.

Peter sensed my own pain and confusion and did something that surprised the hell out of me...and maybe even him, too. He reached out and hugged me...only it wasn't any kind of hug I'd felt before.

It was then that I knew.

That I knew.

We were sitting on his couch, holding hands.

We had been sitting like this for some time. Ten minutes, perhaps. Maybe longer. We were both dealing with a lot of shit.

"My daughter...she came to you in a dream?"

"Yes. I believe so."

"Did she...did she look okay?"

"She did."

He inhaled deeply, although I didn't hear any actual air passing over through his open mouth. His hand, I noted, was soft and pulsated with energy. If my eyes had been closed and I had been asked to describe what I was touching, I would have said a pile of cotton, with a soft electrical current passing through it.

He said, "I haven't seen my daughter since the morning I left for work two years ago." He motioned toward the kitchen before us. "I kissed her forehead there, but she didn't kiss me back. She had stuck out her lower lip. She always did that when she was mad. I had, of course, taken her mother's side of their silly argument and my baby girl was mad at me. I had ruffled her hair and laughed and told her I loved her. At least...at least, I said that." He shook his head sadly. "You know, for someone losing his memory, I sure remember every detail of that day. It's all I have, in a way. It's my last memory of her alive."

"I'm sorry you had to go through this, Peter."

"I'm more sorry for her. And angry. So angry. I want to kill the bastard all over again. I want to kill him a million times, each death more painful than the last."

His words hit me hard and as his discordant energy crackled through me. I tried to forget the man lying on the concrete, gasping and drowning in his own blood.

Peter looked at me. "And it was definitely her teacher?"

"It was."

"Do we know this for a fact?"

"We will soon."

He nodded. "I met him once, at a parent-teacher conference. He seemed...intense. I almost pulled my daughter from his class. I guess I should have..."

He released my hand and wept into his own. I nearly hugged him, nearly put my arm around him, but I refrained, afraid of what I might feel.

Finally, Peter sat back and nodded and breathed deeply, and this time, I heard a ragged sound pass over his lips. The house, I noted, was absolutely silent. Not even the hum of a refrigerator. It had been unplugged, of course. After all, no one needed it. No one living, at least.

"Peter, how did your wife kill herself?"

"She took a bottle of painkillers."

I nodded. "Did you watch her die, Peter?"

"I did, yes."

"And you did nothing to stop it?"

"No."

"Why not?"

"Her…her pain was so great…she couldn't deal with it anymore, or with Penny not being here. She wasn't holding up well."

"And how were you holding up?" I asked.

"Not much better."

We sat together, our knees almost touching. I noted that I had sunk in much deeper on my side of the couch than he had, although he was a bigger man. He said, after a moment, "My wife wanted to be with Penny again, that it was the only way she could be happy."

Peter didn't bother brushing away the silvery tears that now ran down his cheeks.

"But I stayed behind. I had to find the killer. I couldn't let that piece of shit walk the Earth a free man."

I studied Peter Laurie as he spoke, noting the same black suit, the same haircut, the same slightly askew tie. I noted the same scuff on his right shoe. Mostly, I noted the way the air crackled when he was near. I had thought it was because I was feeling his dead wife's energy, or even his daughter's energy. I had, of course, been dead wrong.

I said, "You stayed behind while your wife moved on."

He nodded. More tears spilled free.

"Except you're not telling me everything, are you, Peter?"

He buried his face in his hands and shook his head.

"The two of you, in fact, killed yourselves together?" I said. "Didn't you?"

CHAPTER TWENTY-NINE

Peter wavered in and out of existence.
It was the first time I'd seen him do that. One moment he was there, and the next he wasn't, just a ghostly hint. And, unlike, Millicent, Peter Laurie was very much a ghost.

Finally, face still buried, he nodded. "Yes. We took the pills together, died together, although she went first."

"You watched your wife die?"

"She died in my arms."

"And then you died, too."

"Yes, I suppose so."

"What happened next?" I asked.

"Time passed, although I don't know how long. A day perhaps. I continued sitting near the bed while our bodies lay unmoving, dead. I was alone. Wherever my wife had gone, I didn't know. But I was alone, as I have been since that day." He looked at me. "Until you."

"Do others see you?"

"Let's just say I've scared off one or two potential home buyers." He chuckled lightly.

"You didn't want the house to be sold," I said.

"Not then...but now...now, I don't know what to do."

Detective Smithy had, of course, finally filled me in about the family's tragedy. He had known all along that Peter had committed suicide with his wife, but had played along with hopes that the case might finally be cracked. Mostly, he thought I was crazy, but wanted to see where all of this might lead. After all, the case had been cold for two years, and in came a crazy woman who claimed to have been hired by the deceased father.

Smithy had admitted to me in the parking lot at Clover Field Elementary that he'd been too dumbfounded to say much of anything. Most important, he admitted to dreaming about Peter Laurie the night before our first meeting. Although he had dismissed the dream at the time, when I had come into the office asking if Peter had contacted him, the detective, who was, amazingly, open to the idea of a spirit world, had taken that as a sign. Good for him.

Which led me back to Millicent. She would have known that her son was dead, but she had withheld that information, too. As I sat there and looked at her son's confused face—her dead son's face—I heard her words all over again: "Help my son."

Why she had kept me in the dark, I didn't know. How, exactly, she wanted me to help her dead son, I didn't know that either. But I had some ideas...and it had to do with more than just helping her son find the killer.

Millicent had often told me that those in spirit can only help so much, that many of us must find our own paths, too. Although dead, Peter was still very much mired in the physical world.

Help my son...

Yes, I knew what she needed from me, although I did not think I was the right person for the job. Who was I, after all, other than a part-time Psychic Hotline operator?

Later, after my cry-a-thon, I called Peter's real estate agent, and got the lowdown about the house, too. Peter Laurie's siblings had spent the better part of nine months fighting over the home, until they'd finally come to some agreement. The house, meanwhile, had sat empty for nearly a year. Yes, there had been some interest, but buyers, in general, were not very excited to get involved in a home where a double suicide had occurred.

"Besides," the agent had admitted, lowering her voice conspiratorially, "the house is...creepy. I always feel like someone's watching me. I think the place is haunted."

I asked why she thought that, and she said, "One time, I saw a man in a suit standing at the top of the stairs. But when I looked again, he was gone. To this day, I will not go in that house alone. I make my husband go with me, but he's just as afraid as I am. Two scaredy cats!"

The man—the spirit, the entity, the ghost—sitting next to me was not someone or some*thing* to fear. He was a father hurting, a father lost, a father looking for answers.

"Why did you call me?" I asked Peter suddenly, as we continued sitting together in the darkening room. That I was sitting next to a ghost in an abandoned old house should have sent me running. I wasn't running. Not now or ever.

"I...didn't know who I was calling, truth be known. I found an ad in the Yellow Pages, circled in red ink. I called the number, and got you."

"You can use the phone?"

"I have become quite adept at physical manifestations, as you can see. I can hold this shape for quite a long time."

"How did you find the ad?" I asked.

He thought about that, blinking rapidly...and I briefly wondered if this was just a *memory* of blinking. After all, why did a ghost need to blink, or breathe, or wear clothes, for that matter? He said, "The Yellow Pages had been opened on the counter."

"Who opened it?"

"Why, I don't know. Does it matter?"

"No," I said, thinking of Millicent. "It doesn't. Not now. Why didn't you tell me, Peter?"

"That I was dead?"

"Yes."

He laughed lightly. "Would you have helped a ghost? Or even taken me seriously? And, quite frankly, half the time, I don't remember that I'm dead. I'm losing my memory rapidly, you see. Forgetting who I am, why I'm here. Half the time, I call out to my wife and baby girl, thinking they're here with me. A dozen times over, I've broken down all over again when I remember they are both dead."

Jesus, I thought.

"Do you ever see them, too?"

"My wife and baby girl? No, never. I feel them sometimes. I think I see them sometimes. My mother, too. But when I look again, they're gone."

I thought of the irony: ghosts haunting ghosts. Or, as Millicent would sternly point out, spirits.

Speaking of which, I noted that Millicent was oddly absent. I suspected I knew why…she could only interfere with her son to a point. Perhaps it was the same with his wife and child. They could only influence so much.

It was up to the living to help the lost return home.

It was, in fact, up to me.

CHAPTER THIRTY

"So, what will you do now?" I asked.

We'd been sitting quietly again, as the house grew colder. This had been the longest I'd been with Peter, and I couldn't help but notice he was wavering in and out of existence. One moment, he was as real as any man, and the next he was just a ghostly, wispy specter. I tried not to let it freak me out, but it did a little.

"Now?" he asked. "What do you mean?"

"Now that the killer has been found, you can...move on, right?"

Truth was, I didn't know a whole lot about what I was talking about. I wasn't a medium, although, over these past few weeks, I'd certainly seen my share of spirits and ghosts. But I knew that spirits moved on to...somewhere. They had to. According to Millicent, she and I had been reborn together throughout time and space. And Samantha Moon, too. A kind of soul-mate trifecta. I liked that.

He shook his head, briefly disappeared, reappeared, then said, "Oh, I'm not going anywhere, Allison. I'm perfectly happy staying right here, thank you very much."

"But why here?"

"This is where I last saw my daughter, and where I last saw my wife. This house is full of their stuff and full of their memories. I'll let you in on a little secret, Allison," he said and raised his index finger to his lips. The gesture was oddly wooden. He continued, "I have no intention of moving on. I'm staying right here, and I'll be damned if anyone is going to move in here and take over my daughter's stuff."

Help my son...

Millicent's words again, and I wondered if she thought them to me now, or if they were still bubbling up from my memory.

Probably a little of both.

I wasn't sure how to proceed. I wasn't sure how to convince a ghost that it was in his best interest to leave behind all that he knew and loved and to venture off into what I saw as the Great Unknown.

I didn't know, but I knew it was the right thing to do.

So, I did what I do best. I opened my mind and reached out for an answer, hoping like hell one would come to me.

As we sat together, as Peter sat forward on the couch, his back straight, rigid and unmoving, I had a brief vision of a golden tunnel with glorious light pouring out. And just as quickly, the vision disappeared.

I asked Peter about the tunnel, and he said, "Ah, yes, the tunnel. I've seen it often, although it comes less and less these days. When it does come, I ignore it."

"What do you mean *when it comes*? What does it look like?"

He pointed toward the vaulted ceiling high above even the second floor, which rose up into a sort of rounded, windowed dome. Yes, a nice house. "I see it up there. It's full of light. Sometimes, I can see people inside, but mostly I feel the light. It feels warm."

"You are warm?"

He shook his head and his body rippled slightly as energy wavered. "No. I'm cold. Always cold."

"Don't you want to be warm, Peter?"

He nodded, thought about it, then shook his head vigorously. "I failed my daughter, Allison. I allowed this happened to her, you see? And then I lost my wife, too. I'm not losing their things, too. It's the last I have of them."

"They are more than things, Peter."

"I know. But it's all I have—"

"What if they are waiting for you in the tunnel?"

"And what if they aren't, Allison? What if I move on and there's…nothing?"

I had no argument to that, but then words appeared in my thoughts, perhaps supplied to me by Millicent herself. I said, "Moving on takes great faith, Peter."

"Perhaps, but I'm not willing to find that out. I will stay right here, with their stuff, with their memory. I can't leave their stuff behind, Allison. I just can't let it be thrown out, or forgotten."

This was, of course, the key, and I had missed it before. "What if I promise to keep all of it for you? I will hang your daughter's paintings, too. In my home, in the homes of my friends. She will never be forgotten."

He looked at me sideways, wavered in and out of existence, and I saw the tears in his eyes. "You would do that for my baby girl?"

"Of course," I said. "She's very talented."

"Yes, I would like that—no, no I can't. I just can't leave them behind. I can't do it. I'm sorry. I know your intentions are good…"

He gasped, and the energy around him crackled. And around me, too. The hair on my neck and arms stood on end. Crackling living light swarmed through the room—and briefly illuminated dead light bulbs.

Holy smokes, I thought.

"It's okay, Peter. I'm not making you do anything. You can stay here as long as you want."

The crackling energy, after a moment, abated. Peter seemed to relax a little, too. An agitated ghost was not a pretty thing to see. I tried to hide the fact that I'd nearly peed myself.

Help my son…help my son…help my son…

I heard Millicent's words again and again, and this time, I wasn't so sure they were a flash of memory. I suspected that Peter was at a crossroads here. He would either go now, or perhaps never. And Millicent wasn't going to let that happen.

Peter snapped his head up, looking past me. I saw a bright glow in his eyes. I turned and looked, too…but saw nothing.

I looked back at him, and the unearthly glow was still there. "It's here, isn't it, Peter?"

He nodded slowly, and continued staring up.

CHAPTER THIRTY-ONE

"Can you see anyone inside?" I asked.
"Yes, a few people."
"Do you recognize them?"
He shook his head. "They're just shadows, shapes."
"What else do you see?"
"An opening in the ceiling, bright white light pouring through. Silhouettes beyond."
"Where does the tunnel lead to, Peter?"
"I don't know."

Millicent, I thought, frustrated. *Where are you? I need your help.*

You're doing fine, child.

I can't do this alone! I don't know what I'm doing!

You're not alone, dear. We are all here. Watching, waiting, helping. And, yes, you do know what you're doing. My boy needs to take the first step. Peter needs to do that on his own. That first step.

And then what?

And then we will show him Heaven.

Are you there with his wife and daughter?

I am.

I turned back to Peter. He was still looking up, mouth slightly open, eyes aglow. He flicked into and out of existence, and there was a very real possibility that Fletcher really had hit me in a parking lot, and I was dreaming all of this, perhaps one last hallucination for a dying brain.

Perhaps, but for now, I had either a real ghost or a made-up ghost that needed to go home...wherever home was.

Heaven, dear, came Millicent's voice. *Always Heaven.*

I took Peter's hand. He pulled his gaze down from above and focused on me, although I could still see a ghostly light reflecting in them. Good God, was I looking into Heaven?

"Your daughter is waiting for you," I finally said.

He opened his mouth. I sensed he wanted to say, "You lie," but thought it improper. Instead, he settled for, "I'm afraid you don't know that for sure, Allison."

He had me there. "No, I don't, but I think you know she is. I think you can feel her, Peter."

"I...I don't know what I feel."

"Your mother is there, too. And so is your wife. They're all waiting for you, Peter."

He was shaking his head as I spoke, "My baby girl is gone... they're all gone. All that remains of them is here, in this house... I can't leave them."

"Your mother is telling me they're waiting for you, Peter, but it's up to you to take that first step."

"No, I can't leave..."

As I spoke, I listened to Millicent's words, and repeated them for Peter: "She's telling me that your time here is done, that there is nothing more for you to do here. She says you are her Pistol Pete and she loves you and wants you to come home."

When I said his nickname, he buried his face in his hands and sobbed. "I can't leave them, I can't. I'm all they have..."

I continued, "She says you did a courageous thing by helping catch Penny's killer. But your work here is done. It's time to come home, Peter. Time to heal. Time to find yourself again, Peter. Time to see your daughter. She's waiting for you there, eagerly. Excitedly."

"My baby..." he said between sobs. "I don't know what to do, Allison..."

"Take that first step, Peter."

He lowered his hands and the light in his eyes grew brighter.

"The tunnel is getting closer, isn't it?" I asked.

He nodded. "It's...it's right behind you, Allison. But I don't see them. I don't see anyone..."

Millicent was quiet and so I spoke from the heart: "You need to do it, Peter. On your own. You need to let go of the physical. You need to move on, and they will be waiting for you."

"You promise?"

I opened my mouth, closed it, then nodded. "Yes, I promise."

He wiped his eyes. His hands, I saw, were shaking, and now I could see *through* him completely. He looked at me. "I'm scared, Allison."

I could finally feel it, too: love wafting through me and over me and around me. Love from Millicent, his daughter, his wife, from God.

"There's a lot of love waiting for you, Peter. Your daughter is there. She wants her daddy."

Except Peter wasn't looking at me anymore. He was looking over my shoulder.

I refused to turn around. Instead, I looked into his fading eyes where I could see the glowing reflection of something truly out of this world.

"And you'll watch over my daughter's paintings?" he asked, still looking beyond me.

"I'll find a home for every one of them."

"I would like that. I will never forget your help, Allison."

"And I'll never forget you, Peter."

He looked at me now, for a final time, and gave me a crooked grin. "No, I don't suppose you will."

And with that, he took a step forward...and I watched his eyes light up, and in them, I saw the reflection of a little girl running toward him, arms outstretched.

He smiled broadly and wept and opened his arms wide...and faded away.

The End

Allison returns in:

THE WITCH AND THE ENGLISHMAN
The Witches Trilogy: Book 2

Available now!
eBook * Paperback
Audio Book

Also available:

WITCH TO CHOOSE
A Love Triangle With a Magical Twist
Heart of a Witch Series #1
by H.T. Night

Available now!
eBook

Also available:

MERCY'S MAGIC
The Witch Mysteries #1
by P.J. Day and Elizabeth Basque

Available now!
eBook

Also available:

MOON DANCE
Vampire for Hire #1
by J.R. Rain

Moon Dance is available at:
eBook * Kobo * Nook

CHAPTER ONE

I was folding laundry in the dark and watching Judge Judy rip this guy a new asshole when the doorbell rang.

I flipped down a pair of Oakley wrap-around sunglasses and, still holding a pair of little Anthony's cotton briefs in one hand, opened the front door.

The light, still painfully bright, poured in from outside. I squinted behind my shades and could just make out the image of a UPS deliveryman.

And, oh, what an image it was.

As my eyes adjusted to the light, a hunky guy with tan legs and beefy arms materialized through the screen door before me. He grinned at me easily, showing off a perfect row of white teeth. Spiky yellow hair protruded from under his brown cap. The guy should have been a model, or at least my new best friend.

"Mrs. Moon?" he asked. His eyes seemed particularly searching and hungry, and I wondered if I had stepped onto the set of a porno movie. Interestingly, a sort of warning bell sounded in my head. Warning bells are tricky to discern, and I automatically assumed this one was telling me to stay away from Mr. Beefy, or risk damaging my already rocky marriage.

"You got her," I said easily, ignoring the warning bells.

"I've got a package here for you."

"You don't say."

"I'll need for you to sign the delivery log." He held up an electronic gizmo-thingy that must have been the aforementioned delivery log.

"I'm sure you do," I said, and opened the screen door and stuck a hand out. He looked at my very pale hand, paused, and then placed the electronic thing-a-majig in it. As I signed it, using a plastic-tipped pen, my signature appeared in the display box as an arthritic mess. The deliveryman watched me intently through the screen door. I don't like to be watched intently. In fact, I prefer to be ignored and forgotten.

"Do you always wear sunglasses indoors?" he asked casually, but I sensed his hidden question: *And what sort of freak are you?*

"Only during the day. I find them redundant at night." I opened the screen door again and exchanged the log doohickey for a small square package. "Thank you," I said. "Have a good day."

He nodded and left, and I watched his cute little buns for a moment longer, and then shut the solid oak door completely. Sweet darkness returned to my home. I pulled up the sunglasses and sat down in a particularly worn dining room chair. Someday I was going to get these things re-upholstered.

The package was heavily taped, but a few deft strokes of my painted red nail took care of all that. I opened the lid and peered inside. Shining inside was an ancient golden medallion. An intricate Celtic cross was engraved across the face of it, and embedded within the cross, formed by precisely cut rubies, were three red roses.

In the living room, Judge Judy was calmly explaining to the defendant what an idiot he was. Although I agreed, I turned the TV off, deciding that this medallion needed my full concentration.

After all, it was the same medallion worn by my attacker six years earlier.

CHAPTER TWO

There was no return address and no note. Other than the medallion, the box was empty. I left the gleaming artifact in the box and shut the lid. Seeing it again brought back some horrible memories. Memories I have been doing my best to forget.

I put the box in a cabinet beneath the china hutch, and then went back to Judge Judy and putting away the laundry. At 3:30 p.m., I lathered my skin with heaping amounts of sun block, donned a wide gardening hat and carefully stepped outside.

The pain, as always, was intense and searing. Hell, I could have been cooking over an open fire pit. Truly, I had no business being out in the sun, but I had my kids to pick up, dammit.

So I hurried from the front steps and crossed the driveway and into the open garage. My dream was to have a home with an attached garage. But, for now, I had to make the daily sprint.

Once in the garage and out of the direct glare of the spring sun, I could breathe again. I could also smell my burning flesh.

Blech!

Luckily, the Ford Windstar minivan was heavily tinted, and so when I backed up and put the thing into drive, I was doing okay again. Granted, not great, but okay.

I picked up my son and daughter from school, got some cheeseburgers from Burger King and headed home. Yes, I know, bad mom, but after doing chores all day, I definitely was *not* going to cook.

Once at home, the kids went straight to their room and I went straight to the bathroom where I removed my hat and sunglasses, and used a washcloth to remove the extra sunscreen. Hell, I ought to buy stock in Coppertone. Soon the kids were hard at work saving our world from Haloes and had lapsed into a rare and unsettling silence. Perhaps it was the quiet before the storm.

My only appointment for the day was right on time, and since I work from home, I showed him to my office in the back. His name was Kingsley Fulcrum and he sat across from me in a client chair, filling it to capacity. He was tall and broad shouldered and wore his tailored suit well. His thick black hair, speckled with gray, was jauntily disheveled and worn long over his collar. Kingsley was a striking man and would have been the poster boy for dashing rogues if not for the two scars on his face. Then again, maybe poster boys for rogue did have scars on their faces. Anyway, one was on his left cheek and the other was on his forehead, just above his left eye. Both were round and puffy. And both were recent.

He caught me staring at the scars. I looked away, embarrassed. "How can I help you, Mr. Fulcrum?"

"How long have you been a private investigator, Mrs. Moon?" he asked.

"Six years," I said.

"What did you do before that?"

"I was a federal agent."

He didn't say anything, and I could feel his eyes on me. God, I hate when I can feel eyes on me. The silence hung for longer than I was comfortable with and I answered his unspoken question. "I had an accident and was forced to work at home."

"May I ask what kind of accident?"

"No."

He raised his eyebrows and nodded. He might have turned a pale shade of red. "Do you have a list of references?"

"Of course."

I turned to my computer, brought up the reference file and printed him out the list. He took it and scanned the names briefly. "Mayor Hartley?" he asked.

"Yes," I said.

"He hired you?"

"He did. I believe that's the direct line to his personal assistant."

"Can I ask what sort of help you gave the mayor?"

"No."

"I understand. Of course you can't divulge that kind of information."

"How exactly can I help you, Mr. Fulcrum?" I asked again.

"I need you to find someone."

"Who?"

"The man who shot me," he said. "Five times."

CHAPTER THREE

The furious sounds of my kids erupting into an argument suddenly came through my closed office door. In particular, Anthony's high-pitched shriek. Sigh. The storm broke.

I gave Kingsley an embarrassed smile. "Could you please hold on?"

"Duty calls," he said, smiling. Nice smile.

I marched through my single story home and into the small bedroom my children shared. Anthony was on top of Tammy. Tammy was holding the remote control away from her body with one hand and fending off her little brother with the other. I came in just in time to witness him sinking his teeth into her hand. She yelped and bopped him over the ear with the remote control. He had just gathered himself to make a full-scale leap onto her back, when I stepped into the room and grabbed each by their collar and separated them. I felt as if I had separated two ravenous wolverines. Anthony's fingers clawed for his sister's throat. I wondered if they realized they were both hovering a few inches off the floor. When they had both calmed down, I set them down on their feet. Their collars were ruined.

"Anthony, we do not bite in this household. Tammy, give me the remote control."

"But Mom," said Anthony, in that shriekingly high-pitched voice that he used to irritate me. "I was watching 'Pokemon' and she turned the channel."

"We each get one half hour after school," Tammy said smugly. "And you were well into *my* half hour."

"But you were on the phone talking to *Richaaard.*"

"Tammy, give your brother the remote control. He gets to finish his TV show. You lost your dibs by talking to *Richaaard.*" They both laughed. "I have a client in my office. If I hear any more loud voices, you will both be auctioned off on eBay. I could use the extra money."

I left them and headed back to the office. Kingsley was perusing my bookshelves. He looked at me before I had a chance to say anything and raised his eyebrows.

"You have an interest in the occult," he said, fingering a hardback book. "In particular, vampirism."

"Yeah, well, we all need a hobby," I said.

"An interesting hobby, that," he said.

I sat behind my desk. It was time to change the subject. "So you want me to find the man who shot you five times. Anything else?"

He moved away from my book shelves and sat across from me again. He raised a fairly bushy eyebrow. On him, the bushy eyebrow somehow worked.

"Anything else?" he asked, grinning. "No, I think that will be quite enough."

And then it hit me. I *thought* I recognized the name and face. "You were on the news a few months back," I said suddenly.

He nodded once. "Aye, that was me. Shot five times in the head for all the world to see. Not my proudest moment."

Did he just say *aye*? I had a strange sense that I had suddenly gone back in time. How far back, I didn't know, but further enough back where men said *aye.*

"You were ambushed and shot. I can't imagine it would have been anyone's proudest moment. But you survived, and that's all that matters, right?"

"For now," he said. "Next on the list would be to find the man who shot me." He sat forward. "Everything you need is at your disposal. Nothing of mine is off limits. Speak to anyone you need to, although I ask you to be discreet."

"Discretion is sometimes not possible."

"Then I trust you to use your best judgment."

Good answer. He took out a business card and wrote something on the back. "That's my cell number. Please call me if you need anything." He wrote something under his number. "And that's the name and number of the acting homicide detective working my case. His name is Sherbet, and although I found him to be forthcoming and professional, I didn't like his conclusions."

"Which were?"

"He tends to think my attack was nothing but a random shooting."

"And you disagree?"

"Wholeheartedly."

We discussed my retainer and he wrote me a check. The check was bigger than we discussed.

"I don't mean to be rude," said Kingsley as he stood and tucked his expensive fountain pen inside his expensive jacket, "but are you ill?"

I've heard the question a thousand times.

"No, why?" I asked brightly.

"You seem pale."

"Oh, that's my Irish complexion, lad," I said, and winked.

He stared at me a moment longer, and then returned my wink and left.

ABOUT THE AUTHOR

J.R. Rain is an ex-private investigator who now writes full-time in the Pacific Northwest. He lives in a small house on a small island with his small dog, Sadie, who has more energy than Robin Williams.

Please visit him at www.jrrain.com.
Add him on Facebook.
Add him on Twitter.

Made in the USA
Lexington, KY
02 May 2016